# Bitter Fig

Kristin Wall

# DEDICATION

To my father and his beloved memory

# ACKNOWLEDGMENTS

Thank you to all my Sunday School teachers over the years and to my Bible teachers at my Christian elementary schools for their inspirational instruction.

# CHAPTER ONE

*Vale of Siddim, City of Gomorrah, about 1867 BCE*
As Lilliana tended to the offerings at the altar filled with the best fruits from the harvest, a shiver ran up her spine. She shook off the sensation.

The temple lay silent and empty in this inner chamber that only the initiated high priest and high-priestess entered. Daily oblations were made for the City of Gomorrah and the lands roundabout. The bounty then fed the poorest citizens who were gathering for the evening meal.

Lilliana listened to the silence, a sense of disquiet coming over her again as she conducted her duties. While she arranged the offerings on the altar, she admired its molded animals along its sides painted in brilliant shades. She started humming to herself.

The torch's lights danced across the painted walls when she saw the shadow creep across the temple's inner room.

The shape of a knife hovered midair…

Her heart pounded with the realization. She held her breath as she grasped the engraved ceremonial dagger from the altar. Meant to scatter evil spirits, she sliced it through the air as she whirled. The sound of footsteps and her extra senses had alerted her, and now she gasped as she faced off the intruder to the sacred space.

The attacker stopped behind her at the sight of the weapon. Clothed in richly dyed robes, a black hood over his face, he wielded a long hunting knife. He whispered in a sinister tone, "Give me the coffers and no one gets hurt."

Lilliana parried. Side stepping his deadly thrust belying his words, she hissed, "you can't take the god's offerings."

"He won't be using it this day, and you won't either."

"You want the offerings?" she shuffled closer to the bowl of figs on the altar, and grabbed a fistful of them. "You want the offerings? Fine, take the fruit that will be fed to the poor of the city." She threw the figs at his face, but he bucked forward, the figs sliding off.

He jumped at her and landed near enough for her to feel his fetid breath.

Ducking sideways, she came up with a kick to his middle. She heard a satisfying grunt behind the mask.

He doubled over for a moment.

He stabbed at her extended leg, and the ceremonial purple robe rent. Lilliana felt a searing pain, but as the attacker was bent to reach for the attack, she struck the back of his neck with the ancient dagger with its zig-zag blade.

He crumpled with an oath, then fell to the stone floor. Blood seeped through his disguise, and she stepped backwards, bumping into the altar.

Dislodged fruit tumbled onto the smooth floor.

"Guard!" Lilliana broke the sacred silence that overlaid the temple at this time of day as she shouted. She waited, listening for his approach.

The sound of running steps approached in the hallway a minute later.

"High priestess," the guard said, suddenly angered as he slid to a halt and viewed the scene. "What have you done?"

"Yes, Nodin, I've shed blood in the Temple." She laid the bloodied dagger back onto the golden altar.

"There will be a curse on you from it," he spat out in a tone that said she should know better.

"I know what is said about the curses. It is you who disrespect the temple by presuming I have no right to defend myself here."

Grunting, the guard bent to examine the corpse that still twitched. He rolled it over onto its back and pulled the black hood off of it.

Lilliana gasped in horror. "It's the governor's son." It was worse than she'd thought. The governor was arguably the most powerful man in the city besides the king. In times past, it had been the high priest who wielded the most power, but of late the faith of the inhabitants had suffered. The governor's power had increased in the uncertainty. Like other nobles of Gomorrah, he had his own private army that kept the city in a choke hold.

They both stared, immobilized at the sight of his youngest son lying dead on the floor.

Frankincense from the corners of the room wafted on the air to them in the silence as the guard examined the dead man. Nodin lifted the dead man's hair on his neck to examine the death blow, and Lilliana observed with shock that she'd stabbed through the tattooed mark of his secret order.

The Order of Godolfin. She'd only heard rumors of it, until now. But she'd seen it's emblem before. The king had warned the temple clergy of the new prophet claiming to be the new hand of El, their city's patron deity. He'd forged an order that was rumored to be about many things that were illegal. Everyone knew of its deadly nature. And here was one of its own, a powerful son who'd just tried to murder her. She shuddered.

"This will go hard on you," Nodin said with certainty as he rose.

Lilliana of course knew that the occult order's symbol of the medallion of the Order of Godolfin that was marked on the man's neck bode ill. Everyone feared the group that was rumored to run the underworld of the City of Gomorrah and some said also the other cities of the Vale of Siddim. All done by foul means.

"I suppose … " the guard hesitated, his broad shoulders shrugging.

"What is it?" Lilliana slumped in resignation. She examined her cut leg. Blood

4

seeped, soiling the exquisite cloth as it dripped to the smooth limestone floor. Now that she was paying attention to it, it stung. She'd need to have it stitched by the look of it. She sighed.

"I could hide the body, then no one will be the wiser." He stared hard at her, then he nodded. "It's for the best. That's what I'll do. It's better if no one finds out. It'll be our secret that stays within this temple."

His loyalty was touching. Suddenly it seemed the wisest choice. The Order was deadly, even if this one of its members had failed. She'd never known them to defile the Temple before now. But these were foul times for the city. The poor were growing in number, the slaves were uprising, and the nobles had walled themselves into an inner-city in order to avoid the main occupants of Gomorrah. These were hardened times that called for drastic measures. "Where can you hide it?" she asked.

"There is a slough," he said under his breath as he grasped the body and hefted it with a loud grunt. Blood ran down his blue painted leather and metal armor. "The sun will set soon. I can get through the city after dark."

"Perhaps you should take another guard with you."

A noise at the entrance to the inner chamber alerted her. A crowd had gathered. Her shout must've alerted them. It was a group of the poor who'd been awaiting their daily evening meal outside. They'd broken the rules to come inside and satisfy their curiosity. Surprise grabbed her, then fear followed it. This was bad.

"We have witnesses," Lilliana said in a low voice and wiped her blood-splattered hand on her purple robe. "I don't think we can keep this just our secret."

"Then I suppose the king can protect you," the guard surmised, but he sounded doubtful as he dropped the body back onto the stone floor.

The king was her brother, and because of that, she'd been installed as the high priestess of El. The temple ran the City of Gomorrah for all practical purposes, at least on the surface when it came to handling work regimens and daily commerce practices. But lately, undercurrents of pure evil had been running through the city and the temple had more to worry about than transactions. It had become a haven amid the chaos. But could she hide this?

"I am the innocent one here. I shouldn't have to worry about this act of self-defense," she said with more bravado than she felt. "These people can be prevailed upon to keep quiet." She turned to the small crowd expectantly. The faces that met her gaze unsettled her.

The guard guffawed. "Don't be naïve. In any other valley, it would be as you say. But you have slain the governor's last born. The same governor who inherited the office and whose sons will follow him."

"I am in the right. The Assembly will defend me."

"The Assembly is as corrupt as the governorship. You have been too insulated here in

El's temple if you think that."

Lilliana cowered at the thought. "I have to do something." A finger of fear began to work its way up her spine, and she shivered. Her leg also stung from where the attacker's blade had struck her. Distracted, she glanced downward and noted dispassionately that the trickle of blood soaking her rent robe was dripping onto the temple floor still.

The guard kicked at the body on the floor.

"Ask and I will do as you say, High Priestess." He bent low in abiesance. "I will do your bidding on this matter. I've already proposed one solution."

"Then clear the temple, and we will discuss this further." She must have courage, and she straightened to her full height.

"I have stopped a thief and a killer," Lilliana explained to the onlookers.

They stared back at her.

Pushing through the gathered crowd, the temple manager stepped into the inner chamber. "What has occurred here? Who dares to desecrate this temple? What has happened?"

He hissed. As he listened to Nodin's explanation, he stumbled, "wha-what c-can I do?"

"Falal-gitu," Lilliana explained. "There has been an attack upon my person. I'm lucky to be alive. And he was trying to steal the offerings to El. This man tried to kill me," Lilliana said. "Please help the guard remove the vile form from this sacred site. We must attend to this matter right away."

"You will need to beseech the patron god for

forgiveness of this degradation," Falal-gitu said as he stroked his beard absently.

"Don't lecture me. I will worry about that later. But for now …" she replied, pushing at the corpse with her sandaled foot. "For now, I have to get rid of…"

"Then I will help you," he said sullenly. "Only because I know you to be honorable and there must be a plausible explanation."

"Indeed," she sighed, wiping at blood splatter on her purple robe. She needed to go change into another one so that she could carry on with the evening rituals. It was better to get on with things as quickly as possible.

"I will get a rug to roll the body in so that it can be passed," the manager decided.

Nodin nodded and lugged the body behind the broad altar to hide it from view, then snapped to attention, his armor and helmet catching the light from the torches on the walls. "I will have to bribe the witnesses."

Lilliana frowned, coming to a quick decision. "Then take it from the same coffers this attacker tried to rob." As high priestess she was in charge of the temple and could hide the missing amounts. It would only add to her errors this night, but it wasn't to be helped.

She walked behind the altar to a stone alcove that held the bronze bowl with the day's best offerings. Picking it up, she carried it to the guard. "It's better this way."

The guard talked with the dozen witnesses who stared at Lilliana with a variety of emotions playing across their faces. He gave them gruff orders to not disclose what they saw, and he handed them each a handful of jewelry and gems from the bowl. Greed lit up their eyes, and heads began to nod. Lilliana decided they were happy to be getting many weeks' worth of income from the bribe. It wouldn't be funds that she would have to account for that would be missed by the temple but these poor had gathered for the daily feeding from the temple grounds. They'd also come to find work which the temple doled out to those who came by, but it was too late in the day for that today.

She shook her head, watching the crowd disperse. What was niggling at her was a rising concern that the secret occult society of the attacker would come after her. Her life was now in danger.

The guard was right, the body would have to be hidden.

It would buy her some time.

The temple manager reentered, dragging a long rug that he began to roll the body into. The temple high-priest, Tamru, rushed into the chamber.

"What is this travesty?" he exclaimed.

"It is a killer who tried to steal the god's coffers." Lilliana indicated her bleeding leg. "He didn't succeed."

"But you have shed blood in the temple," Tamru rubbed his head shaved in the Egyptian style.

"I had no choice. It was self-defense."

"The Goddess should've shown you a different solution. But since she didn't," he bent over as he spoke, helping to roll the body into the rug. "I will help hide the evidence."

"And I'll clean up the blood," the manager added.

"No one speak of this," Lilliana implored as the small gathering began to disperse, clutching at their new treasures.

The task was done quickly, and Lilliana found herself alone again. She looked at her leg, which she'd have to attend to before she stained the temple further. But she worried that the worse mark would be an unseen one.

There was a solution. She would find her brother, the king. Maybe there was something he could do to help her out of this situation; for now she was in danger if the order found out.

She would go to the king. He had not lost so much power that he couldn't help her. He was her hope now.

She would have to wait until morning because her brother would be outside the palace on his nightly foray into the City of Gomorrah's pleasures. He would be back at the palace by morning for his civic duties. She would see him then. For now she needed to attend to her leg.

Back in her bed chamber, Lilliana cleaned her wound and wrapped her leg in a clean cloth. As she tied a knot, she decided which healer to go to in the morning to have her cut sewn together. For now, the cloth had staunched the bleeding. Donning another purple ceremonial robe with gold-thread embroidered borders, she headed back to the inner-chamber, the holy of holies. There, Falal-gitu was cleaning the blood with the help of one of the kitchen workers.

"Will it come clean?" Lilliana asked hesitantly.

"I told you, I will cover this deed, High Priestess," the manager said.

Holding her breath for a count, Lilliana watched, then retrieved a tray of the fruit offerings and took it to the kitchen. It was time to feed the people, and the sooner she got back to her duties, the better. Later, she'd pray to El for forgiveness, and for help keeping her secret. Surely her god would be there for her.

\*\*\*

Lilliana strode under the early dawn light as the marketplace was setting up. The street was wide enough for the king's army to march through twenty abreast. It had been paved with stonework in the high days of the city.

Food scents carried on the temperate breeze assailing her nostrils. Her stomach grumbled for she'd forgotten to eat this morning.

Alongside where she strode, the merchants were beginning to open their carts full of wares. The sides of the main streets were lined with crowded carts vying for location to be in proximity to the merchants' houses which were three- and four-story buildings set back from the road. Lilliana knew the inside of those houses were filled with every imaginable luxury. The merchants in the city of Gomorrah had grown fat and wealthy.

This outer portion of the city close to the

walled city's main gate was already bustling, and soon visitors would be entering the city for the rich wares, despite the inherent dangers.

At the other end of the city, residents of the inner-city would make their way out into this open area to haggle and negotiate for their luxury items or to purchase daily food and supplies. The inner-city walls stood like a bastion in the distance as she meandered through the main street.

She mused ironically that nearly anything could be bought in these markets. Including the unlawful. She shivered.

The coolness of the morning was welcome, as it would soon grow too hot to be outside very long, but many of the vendors would persist. Visitors into the city were filing along the road to begin their purchases. But another crowd was gathering.

Lilliana stopped to watch as slaves marked by their copper collars formed into a large group. Their collars were inscribed with their masters' emblems for identification useful for purchasing items. More of the slaves began to congregate in the center of the street, blocking foot traffic as well as beasts of burden.

A shiver ran through Lilliana, as she saw some of them were equipped with sticks and staffs, useful for herding animals, but these slaves were without livestock. Slaves weren't allowed to congregate, and she felt a shudder at the chanting they began -- an eerie tune. Something about solidarity of their union of slaves. She couldn't quite make out the words. Then a shout emanated, the name Godolfin. And cheers.

Lilliana began to tremble. The hated order had infiltrated the slaves' world and who knew what hazard it would now cause as the organized slaves filled the streets in protest. They chanted for rights that weren't theirs for their three years of extreme servitude under the law. It was a hard lot for them, and for some it was a price they'd paid for extreme debt or breaking the law. Only the king could free a slave. Not even the powerful governor could or the seated Assembly made up of the city's nobility and wealthy merchants.

Some slaves began pounding at the carts on the side of the road as they passed and merchants screamed in outrage. Scuffles broke out. Like a crashing wave, their bodies moved as one in purpose. The next moment, they were involved in hand-to-hand matches with vendors and shoppers. Some of them began tearing off their collars and using them to beat upon their victims.

Lilliana decided to flee the scene of the amassed protestors. She could do nothing here, and didn't think she could have enough influence to calm the growing crowd. This was not the same as when the same slaves came to the temple for meals, or to deliver their masters' offerings. This was a violent act of rebellion. Her heart ached for the innocent bystanders being inexorably drawn into the altercations with the slaves.

"Disperse!" a man in a chariot shouted as he pushed through the crowd. "Stop this now!"

Lilliana turned toward the commotion. As the charioteer spread the crowd with a crack of a whip over their heads, it was followed by soldiers on foot with tall spears waving the governor's colors of red and gold. She could see him now in the chariot, and he suddenly found her with his roaming gaze.

She froze in place. Did he know? Surely it was too soon for him to have learned of his son's disappearance. No one who had seen it would've told it after the bribes, surely.

But then he smiled slowly, and she forced herself to calm.

He continued to crack his whip over the heads of the combatants. From the outer edges of the slaves, the governor's personal army was dominating them. When some refused to relent, the soldiers drew their other weapons and began taking lives. The governor circled.

He aimed his chariot toward her now, coming alongside her even as the melee dispersed slowly.

"It's only a small demonstration, High Priestess," he said in a hoarse voice.

"I am grateful." She inclined her head. "A blessing upon your head for this," she blessed him.

He smiled gratefully and swiped at his brow where his circlet sat and he straightened it awkwardly. "There may be even bigger trouble soon. You should take precautions."

An even greater civil rebellion was fomenting within the city by all accounts, but the king was having trouble recruiting the troops he needed from the city, itself. But the governor appeared fearless, if ignorant of her crime last night against his family. He nodded his head in return, his organized curls bobbing about his head under the bronze circlet of his rank. Then, thankfully, he was pulling away and turning the chariot back to meld with his private soldiers at their work.

Scanning the group of protestors before she turned and strode away, she recognized some of them from the feeding times at the temple. Daily offerings were shared amongst the poor who came begging. Perhaps later she could ask some the regular ones what they were protesting about. But not in the heat of the moment.

She let her legs carry her away at a brisk pace, shaken.

She reminded herself she was on her way to see the king, and hurried away from the approaching throng of noisy shoppers returning after the slaves' rebellious scene.

She decided to hurry. Dust rose up as she stretched her stride under the brightening day. The king's palace would be safe from rebels and street criminals, it being central in the inner-city sequestered behind its own wall.

But the king's power wasn't absolute, and had been growing weaker by the day. The kingship was by heredity but supported by the Assembly made up of the most powerful merchants and nobility. The common people answered to their representatives on the Assembly. It was an old system that she was unsure would hold on much longer.

Her brother the king was also graced to stay in power by the Elamites, by a long ago war treaty, but he was of a mind to declare himself sovereign and rid himself of the foreign power. As of yet, he didn't have the forces in place to enforce it; his private army wasn't strong enough.

All the nobles had their own military forces, and the city had been growing with new factions that were undeclared in their loyalties and open to the highest bidder. It had become a feudal vale. The king hoped to gather enough support, but this recent attack in the temple bode ill for his aspirations because it showed a disregard for the power system in place, and now with an open slave protest. And if the Order was growing so bold....

The king was in danger of being overthrown at any moment. She wasn't certain at all that he'd be able to help her out of her debacle. Still, she'd have to approach him and she wended her way through the side alleys to avoid the crowds even though it was slightly longer to get there. Sporadically, she looked over her shoulder as she slowed her walk.

She had tried to find the king last night, after the late night attack, but he'd been gone about the city attending parties, as was typical. He was single and loved to carouse, holding out for a fortuitous marriage offer from one of the neighboring city-states or kingdoms. He spent long hours in the palace receiving visitors and supplicants by day. She knew she'd find him there by dawn.

The limestone palace emerged as she rounded a corner from an alley and entered through the double-doored gateway into the inner-city. The sunlight warmed the hues of the palace's stark facade. People were already filed into lines outside the elaborate entryway, awaiting. She pushed through them, calling out her rank to gain access past the crowd. The armed guards at the carved doorway ushered her in.

Her embossed decorated leather sandals were covered in dust and she shook them off at the entrance, dipping a ceremonial cloth into the scented water and wiping her feet off before proceeding barefoot into the king's throne room.

Lilliana approached her brother in the reception chamber where he was holding his early morning audience. The limestone walls of his palace were covered in ornately painted frescoes of the wild animals in the region, and a few mythical ones that had perhaps once walked the Vale of Siddim. There were all manner of beasts with wings and horns that filled the tales told to children in Gomorrah, including some frightening ones that were intended to keep the young in line.

She hovered, eyeing the loyal imperial guards lining either side of the great hall. She waited only as long as the supplicant immediately before her.

"King Birsha," Lilliana interrupted his concentration as he he stood and awaited, leaning against his carved stone throne. He'd been pacing about and had seen her enter. He was in the middle of proclaiming his declarations for the supplicant before to the scribe seated by the dais. He was an energetic man, and seldom sat for long. But he held long audiences past the customary times. Lilliana thought his dedication was admirable and she smiled tentatively.

The king looked up at her and graced her with a broad grin. "My favorite sister."

"Your only sister," Lilliana rebuked gently.

The king stroked his plaited dark beard and squinted. His eyes were the same hazel shade as hers.

The guards along the walls stepped forward to silently move the line of supplicants back to the entrance as Lilliana approached her brother.

"I have an urgent matter," she said as she bowed low before him.

He straightened to his full height and bid her, "Rise, my sister and come sit on the throne with me."

The wide throne accommodated the two of them as she sat down on its silk cushion and leaned over to whisper in his ear, "I have killed a man."

His eyebrows rose, then he smiled again.

The scribe next to him worked quickly to record their conversation on a piece of papyrus from Egypt with a sharp stylus, but Lilliana signaled Birsha to halt the recording.

He ordered the scribe, "Stop recording and remove yourself."

"But," he argued. "I'm authorized to hear everything and record it."

"Do as I tell you," King Birsha said. Then more reasonably, "this is a family matter."

"I depart under protest," the royal scribe quipped.

As he sent the scribe away, Birsha turned back to her. "That is not such a big problem. Come,

come, tell me what you did."

"The man was one of the Order of Godolfin," she whispered.

A somber look came over his ruddy face. He grew redder. "That is a problem."

"I realize that. But can you help me?" She shifted uncomfortably, and she wrung her hands together.

"It appears I will have to," he said. "No one else can protect you from the assassins of the Order of Godolfin."

"How can you?" She resettled on the cushioned seat, wrapping her arms about herself. Her stomach felt tight with anxiety. If her brother couldn't help her, then she was doomed. She said, "The reach of the Order runs deep. No one knows where their power begins and ends."

"Perhaps because no one knows who they are."

"Yet their power grows daily."

"I will find you a guard that isn't corrupt."

Lilliana's eyebrows raised. "Indeed?"

"Don't look at me that way. It's possible to do."

"Your confidence gives me some hope."

"A new force of mercenaries has arrived in neighboring Sodom, recent from Ur."

"And what of them?" she asked.

"They will follow the custom of guarding the royal cousinhood, having lost their own kingdom. I've summoned them already. They arrive today sometime according to the messenger they sent ahead. We will have more help here at the royal court, and you'll see. I can have you guarded."

"But we don't know these new mercenaries. Are they better than our own imperial guards?"

"They are our cousinhood and they have a powerful priesthood. They worship the god Jehovah according to the messenger. They should be enough to help get this city back under control."

"Not the Hebrews, surely." Lilliana had heard of them. "They worship the wrong god." Lilliana's concern grew. In Gomorrah, the ancient gods were worshipped, and her place in the temple was assured, next to the male high priest. How would the new gods of these visitors from Ur get along with their city deities? "How can you be sure about these Hebrews?"

"They are warriors who have no loyalties within the city-states of the Vale of Siddim."

"And that means you can trust them?" she whispered harshly, doubtful.

"They have three leaders in the neighboring city."

Skeptical, Lilliana asked, "which city?"

"Sodom is where they've been sojourning. I've already invited them. They'll be here soon. Perhaps this morning unless they're late."

"Are they not engaged by King Bera then?"

"He will have to spare some of them. Our problems are worse than Sodom's or the other cities." King Birsha scowled. "I have the superior bloodline and therefore more authority." He waved at the emblem on his throne of the circular serpent swallowing its tail around a cross. "Our blood goes all the way back to father Cain, and therefore we're of the first kingship. That gives me the authority over the other kings of the vale, but you already know that, dear sister."

"King Bera has been honorable on some other accounts, but not all. He may not turn them over to you so easily. Surely he will have demands."

"It will be done. I've decided. I will hire the mercenaries to guard you and to settle this city back to lawful ways as it was in the beginning."

"It's said that there hasn't been true Law in this valley since the gods stopped walking among us." Lilliana referred to their legends before the gods had departed like migrating birds as recorded in the history.

"That has only been ninety years, and the rotations around the sun have continued nevertheless. We haven't been entirely forsaken. They left us their wisdom. Their knowledge of the stars and the workings of the heavens. Their mastery of herbs and true medicine. They've taken care of us, their seed."

The demigods had seeded the royalty and taught them many things, and established their worship, including the ceremonies that Lilliana carried out herself. The prophecy was that the gods would return again sometime in the future.

She shifted on the bench, wrapping her arms around herself as she shivered. She wondered if it would be soon. If they'd still been among the people, she felt certain there would be order in the city still. What had happened to the city since the demigods had departed was loathed by the majority, but wickedness was growing day by day.

She cajoled her brother, "perhaps if we reestablish order in the city as you plan then the gods will return. At least they left us their bloodline. That counts for something."

"It is a good omen that there is a new force coming to this city. You'll see. They'll be useful. It simply calls for more force to bring Gomorrah in line. Then we can have peace again."

"In the meantime, we all have to take more precautions."

King Birsha hugged her suddenly, then popped to his feet.

"Come, come now. I am weary of this day already, and wish to go swimming. Today is the noonday feast of the five stars, anyhow. The city will stop what it's doing to celebrate so you should put this worry out of your mind. You must join me there and I will make the plans for you. You can see that I'm busy with all the supplicants this morning, but I wish for a quick swim to ease the heat of the day."

"Thank you, Birsha." Lilliana stood and planted a kiss on the ball of his cherubic cheek.

"Guards," King Birsha barked. "Gather a contingent to guard the High Priestess Lilliana."

The captain of the guard rushed forward. "Aye."

A disturbance at the entrance to the throne room caused her to look up. Foreigners were entering, and she stood. It was her first glimpse of the Hebrews, for that is surely who they must be. The one in the lead caught her eye, and she felt herself flush as he locked gazes with her and proceeded into the chamber. With a hesitation, Lilliana tore herself away and plunked back down on the cushioned throne and awaited.

# CHAPTER TWO

Ashurta rode the camel draped in the royal finery of the now lost City of Ur. It was a bitter road he travelled as he was loaded with his weapons of war, which had not been sufficient to stop the civil war in Ur before coming to this verdant valley. But he'd followed his royal cousins Abraham and Lot to this valley of affluent cities where they had attained both shelter and meaningful employment. It was small compensation, but as Lot had reminded him, he had to be grateful.

All should be well, now that they were in the valley, yet Ashurta sensed undercurrents that belied that. The king of Sodom had welcomed them with some trepidation, but Lot had called upon the grace of the cousinhood to allow them sanctuary. Now Ashurta had been called to Gomorrah and he'd brought a hundred of the specialized soldiers who'd left Ur with him and a thousand soldiers for them to command in their new city. Their long caravan stretched behind him. They were young single men who'd been training in the art of guerilla warfare, but had had their lives curtailed by the drastic move. Ashurta was no longer a general of a fine fighting force. They were a rag-tag group of warriors without a city-state any longer but they remained in their armor. The rest of the soldiers and their families and servants remained with Abraham in the valley by the River Jordan where he kept the sheep and goats and wagons of valuables, all that remained of his once great wealth in Ur.

Abraham still commanded twenty-thousand soldiers who'd followed him with their families from Ur. On top of Abraham's flocks, his vestige of the wealth he'd once held had been left behind except for what could be carried; they'd taken over the available grazing lands around the foothills of this valley. Twenty-thousand soldiers that were with the prophet-general made for a sizeable group for Abraham to command, but they were all that had been left and hadn't been enough to protect Ur from the takeover. The city had embraced the conquerors, and it had become time to move on to Haran in the north. And now, to the Vale of Siddim.

He glanced back over his shoulder to look over the caravan of battle camels and chariots and horses and donkeys wending its way along the smooth roadway. Looking about, he could almost believe this was a peaceable place.

In truth, it was a magnificent valley more than the equal to the Edin, the glorious and fertile plain of his homeland. Looking about at the cultivation, he begrudgingly admitted it was superior. Here the land was cultivated with tender care and an eye for beauty. He noted as he bobbed along that the valley was cut in unobtrusive patterened channels of water, similar to the irrigation of the barley fields and fig orchards they'd passed through on the way to Sodom. But here on this stretch of the road, there was no produce or other benefit to keeping the land green. It was simply large parklands and private gardens on the estates they passed; there was no reasoning for using all the water other than the sheer beauty of it all. It was quite a sight as they travelled between the two cities.

He glanced back over his shoulder, wondering why they hadn't met other travelers along the route but had nothing to fear. The rest of the caravan he was escorting to Gomorrah was plodding along behind him. Unlike in his homeland, there was no one on the road to harass them. The caravan all displayed the symbol of their god, Jehovah, the red lion on a banner to announce themselves in peacetime as well as in wartime.

The camel spit into the wind, and Ashurta wiped the slobber off of his voluminous travelling robe. It was damned hot and he pulled the white protective hood lower to keep the burning sun off his already deeply tanned skin.

Daniel, his younger brother moved his camel alongside Ashurta who looked over at him expectantly.

"What is it, Daniel?"

"It isn't as populous as we're used to." He waved his hand about. "Who uses all this parkland?"

"But it seems it's even wealthier than where we've been," Ashurta declared. "Look at all those painted houses of three and four stories coming up. They seem to have guards of their own. They're guarding something valuable."

"I wish we hadn't had to leave Haran," Daniel said.

"It is our duty to follow the prophet Abraham." Ashurta took Daniel's loyalty for granted, perhaps as Abraham took his own.

"I know, I know. To the cousinhood. But we aren't beholden to them, nor them to us."

"Not yet," Ashurta said. "But we will be soon enough. There is honorable work for us here."

"The countryside was supporting us in Haran just fine."

"Abraham's wealth could only go so far, little brother. He has a lot of people to support."

"He has sheep enough to support an army."

"Such that is left of it," Ashurta agreed. "But we can't ask him to use it all on us."

Daniel grunted, but remained quiet.

They rode on in amicable silence for a time.

"The River Jordan is going to dry up in this heat," Daniel quipped, dabbing at the sweat on his brow under his bronze helmet lined with wool padding.

Ashurta laughed. "It may, indeed, but for now it makes a fertile plain. Look at all that irrigation. We should do well here." He tried to sound optimistic to bolster his brother who'd doubted this trip from the start and to hide the fact that he was having his own doubts about moving to Canaan. They'd stopped over in the city of Sodom and it hadn't been what he was accustomed to. The city was rich on the surface but wicked undercurrents abounded.

They rode beside the Salt Sea southerly until the city of Gomorrah rose on the horizon, and Ashurta relaxed for the final leg of the short trip. He would need to find an accommodation within the city to clean himself before his visit with his cousin, the king. King Birsha had sent for Lot also. He needed Ashurta for protection, but Lot for matters of state. Although Lot was delayed in his new home of Sodom, he would be coming to visit soon. Ashurta had been convinced to respond to Birsha's request. It bode well to work for the cousinhood after misfortune. There was law enforcement and protective services work awaiting him. After losing his city, it was something. The bloodlines always turned to each other, relying on one another.

He'd brought the contingent of soldiers with him, and pack of animals including horses and the onagers that pulled the war chariots and donkeys to be beasts of burden and of course the battle camels. They might need any of them for inside the city. The caravan with him would need to be accommodated. They may've fled the overtaken city of Ur, but they were seasoned soldiers and had served their prior city-states for years. His men were hardened and jaded despite their youth, but he wanted to see to their comfort right away. To bolster morale that had been flagging. It wasn't helped by the long journey.

The swaying of the camel lulled him, as they approached the city despite his sour thoughts. This was the type of assignment he'd done before. It should be as easy as a honey cake going down.

Thirsty, he reached for his wineskin and took a swig. The sun was still rising, and already he felt the sweat dripping down his torso; he swiped it away from his eyes.

Around him, groves of date trees were flourishing as they approached the city. Workers moved among them, as they would probably until the high heat of the day arrived. No workers or even slaves would be subjected to the high heat of the day, but they quietly worked now. Guards lolled in the shade holding the leads of large thick-set dogs with short hair and square jaws.

He spotted more three-story mud-brick houses between the rows of trees, set back from the roadway. The nobles of the land, no doubt. Soon he spotted more abodes grouped together of one- or two-stories which would be the homes of the poor.

A sudden bird-cry overhead alerted him. Circling vultures heading towards the nearest waterway. Ashurta watched them for a bit until they'd almost ridden past. Something big must've died there. He should investigate, he decided, although it could be anything. His curiosity got to him and he grinned at Daniel beside him.

He turned in his seat and with the wave of an arm, he beckoned the others in his party to continue on and not follow him to the edge of the slough where the vultures were circling.

"Where are you going?" Daniel pressed,

making to follow him.

"Stay here, little brother," Ashurta ordered. "I'm just going to check on this."

As he approached, he saw it was a body lying face up, in an embellished purple robe, swollen from the water. Dismounting, he turned the body over and saw the bloody hole at the neckline. It looked like murder. This was a case of foul play.

He frowned. Someone had died by the hand of another, and with his new position at court he would be responsible for such incidents. Someone had gone through the trouble of depositing the body in the slough, hiding their foul deed.

He might as well start on his new duties to the city with this crime. The king had hired him to bring order back to the city. This was how he'd start.

Loading the dead man over the back hump of his camel, he tied him down and then he rejoined the caravan. They proceeded onward. He had his first order of business as the city's new protector now. He would find the murderer of this man. It was a good place to start.

He spurred the camel onward to the beckoning city, passing through the open gates, the double city walls, and he started staring in wonder at the ornately painted buildings. They passed through a bustling marketplace, with wooden carts lining the wide main street. The camel and the rest of his caravan slowed to a shuffling pace due to the crowd.

People pushed past one another, gathering around the vendor carts where merchants were vying for business. The camels snorted in ire at the people around them. Then Ashurta saw a melee up ahead, and a charioteer with a whip after the rioting crowd. Guards were running up to the altercation, separating some protestors and dragging them away. He slowed his camel to give the melee time to die down. He waited a few minutes until the guards had done their best.

They rode on.

The amber temple rose up above the rest of the city, terraced with greenery planted on its steppes. It was made of limestone that glowed warmly in the noonday sunshine. Behind it was the palace, just visible. The palace was behind a second inner-city wall, creating a fortress within. Ashurta could see that the city was segmented into different echelons. There was an obvious caste system, and he noted groups of slaves working in various capacities nearly everywhere he looked. He scowled, for he disagreed with slavery and thought that better commerce could be achieved without it if cities applied themselves to other solutions. But slavery was lucrative and most cities indulged in it. Still, he'd have a word with King Birsha about it.

Besides all that, based upon the unwelcome looks he and his caravan were getting, foreigners were apparently unwanted here. He gave up on the idea of finding someone friendly with a house where he and Daniel could clean up before arriving at court. He checked over his shoulder to ensure the caravan was staying together. He didn't like the look of this crowd.

On alert, he surveyed the area. Along the

broad thoroughfare were lines of three-story mud-brick houses with vendor carts in front of them. These would be the merchants' homes. Judging by the wealthy raiment all around, he guessed that the merchant homes would also be luxurious. All along the winding road through the first section of the city, large wooden constructions with awnings protected the carts from the sun. A wide variety of offerings were loaded up in the carts. People swarmed among them in a bevy of activity.

Colorful attire of the long protective robes in dyes of vegetables and elaborate embroidery attested to the city's wealth. The attire also greatly included the use of the purple dye the valley was famous for. Ashurta noted that most of the slaves from the melee were men that had shaved heads as if they were marked for the slave class by it. Also denoted by their brief loincloths and copper neck collars which he was sure contained their owner's information. The amount of slaves also proved that Gomorrah was at least as wealthy as its neighboring cities.

He and his small caravan slowed even further to a crawl to navigate through the crowds who did little more than spare them hateful glances, while avoiding the tall camels and bulky charioteers.

At last, they passed through the inner-city gateway and the palace came into view between the tall buildings along the thoroughfare. It was poised on the east side of the city on a hill behind the inner wall, surrounded by canals that watered a profuse flower garden, and towering groves of trees. The palace itself was broad and painted white with carved doorways at the entrance where scores of people were waiting in lines.

Ashurta signaled the camel to kneel so that he could disembark. He slid to the ground, stretching his aching limbs. The others in the caravan lined the streets and did the same, waiting for him to proceed. The caravan was still filing in through the inner-city gate, and it would take them some time to come together at a stop. He would check on them later. Meanwhile, they could water their animals at the garden canals.

Ashurta eyed the lines in front of him and decided not to wait behind them. It was a privilege of his rank. He marched up to the entrance between a row of blue-uniformed imperial guards. Their tunics gleamed with copper embroidery and their bronze weapons and shields gleamed in the morning sun. The stone walkway was covered in dust that the breeze and supplicants carried in and he shook the dust off of his robe that he wore over his armor.

Ashurta stopped at the entrance and announced himself to the guard, then shook the dust off of his sandals. He stopped at the footbath and dipped a white linen swath into the scented water and wiped his feet before proceeding through the tall double-doorway carved with exotic animal motif.

There was a long line of supplicants ahead of him, people from all walks of life, but the captain of the guard approached him and assured him that the king would see him next despite the long line which looked upon him suspiciously. His voluminous robe was different from their own dyed linen attire in riotous colors which bare their upper arms and calves. He noticed it was a style favored by most of the city's upper-class residents showing off their bronzed limbs. Most of the people appeared to have suntans.

He stepped further inside and stood with his feet planted apart and his fists on his hips.

A simmering fury filled him as he listened in on the various crimes the king was passing judgement about. The crimes of the city had to be stopped, and he may as well start with this body he'd retrieved. It was his duty. He frowned, not wanting to wait behind the line of supplicants in the room. He'd been on the road from Sodom all night, after all.

He signaled Daniel who was hovering at the great doorway. "Bring the gift," he said softly. Daniel nodded and went back outside.

Ashurta surveyed the scene with impatience, noting the beautiful woman in a purple robe and glimmering jewelry sitting next to the king on his big throne with her pinned-up hairdo and Egyptian cosmetics. He had trouble removing his gaze from her, noting the shine of her dark hair and the light in her hazel eyes.

He shook himself and came to a decision.

He returned to the line of camels and removed the dead man, hefting him over his shoulder. Marching back into the court, he strode to the throne bypassing the supplicants and tossed the body at the feet of his cousin. The king jumped and the woman sitting next to him, recoiled. She was garbed in a high-priestesses robe, and silver and lapis lazuli jewelry all over her magnificent form. He caught her gaze and watched the stunned horror take over her refined features.

The guards had rushed forward as he tossed the body down onto the tile.

The beautiful priestess jumped up in shock and screamed.

"This is where I begin, oh great King." Ashurta bowed dutifully.

King Birsha scowled. "You must be one of my cousins."

Assured that he'd made his point, Ashurta smiled.

\*\*\*

Lilliana clutched at her throat. The body had been found. How could this be? She shook her head several times in denial, a lock of hair loosening and falling into her face. She blew it away.

She stared at the body for a minute, then tore her gaze away.

This foreign man who looked like an angel avenging a wrong stated, "I'll start with this crime."

"You can't," Lilliana squealed. Her heart thudded painfully. How had he found the body?

"That's the governor's son," someone shouted.

The curious crowd pushed forward, muttering to themselves.

Guards stepped up to push the pressing crowd backwards, barring them with their horizontally held spears.

Lilliana tried again. "You can't."

Beside her, her brother emitted a low chuckle. Damn him for taking this so lightly.

"I am Lord Ashurta of Shinar. I can. And I will," the stranger said. "I'm here to stop these types of things. I'll begin here."

King Birsha stood at a forced ease and walked carefully toward the newly arrived cousin. "You are my cousin, Lord Ashurta. It's good to finally meet you. Welcome to my city."

The two men linked arms, grasping each other's forearms in sudden understanding. Lilliana cocked her eyebrow as she noted they were roughly the same height and build. A family resemblance, she thought.

"I'm ready to get to work on these problems right away. And I'll find out who did this." He puffed up his broad chest, and one of his broad shoulders twitched under his voluminous white robe.

Lilliana bucked up her courage. She believed in truthfulness as a principle, despite her subterfuge last night in collusion with the temple guard and the manager. But the time to confess was not now. In fact, if this Ashurta never found out the truth, the better. The less people who knew, the sooner it could all be forgotten. Her heart thudded painfully as she stared at Ashurta. He was tall and broad in the chest, but the rest she couldn't make out under his open robe. He was handsome in a rugged way with sharp cheekbones and deep blue eyes. He wore no beard, and his hair was long to his shoulders, unlike the cropped hair styles of the local upper-class. She shivered at his fearsome expression.

Ashurta's eyebrows rose as he caught her perusal, but he nodded as the king gave the order to close the chamber against the outsiders. Guards hustled the people out, then positioned themselves by the closed doors.

"And who might you be, grand lady?" Ashurta asked, facing her squarely.

"This is my sister, high priestess Lilliana" Birsha volunteered. "You're both cousins. Do greet each other and forget this little disagreement right now."

"That was an evil man," she pointed to the body.

Ashurta's eyebrows shot upward. "Indeed. How would you know?"

"It's no use trying to investigate such crimes in the city." Stamping her foot, she stepped up to the body of the governor's son. "It would be futile. This city is too far gone." She desperately hoped she could convince him to halt his investigation before it started. She didn't want to face the consequences of anyone further finding out she'd killed the governor's son.

"I make the pronouncements around here," Birsha interjected, planting his fists on his hips. 'I see you don't understand this situation, Ashurta. Lilliana here is in danger already. I need you to focus instead on protecting her. That shall become your primary focus for now. Forget this dead man."

"Excuse me for saying so," he scowled.

"But I'm not partial to simply guarding the spoilt royalty. My efforts will be better placed investigating the crimes and putting a stop to them. It's what I used to do in Ur, before the uprising that is."

"Spoiled?" Lilliana gasped. "I'll have you know that I work very hard in the temple." Lilliana stepped closer to her new cousin, and stared up him. He smelled of camels and sweat, and she wrinkled her nose. It seemed to amuse him. She wondered how she could distract him from this investigation that could only go wrong for her. A knot formed in the pit of her stomach.

"You're standing a little too close to me for propriety, priestess," Ashurta grinned maddeningly.

She stepped back a pace, shuddering at his command tone.

"That'll be enough, you two. Never mind all that," Birsha interjected. "I'll have you know, this is the governor's son, the son of the most powerful man in the city. He has a great following and I'm afraid this will go hard. Add to that the fact that he is marked with the emblem of a secret evil order, and you should be able to comprehend this situation."

A murmur ran through the assembled guards as they looked at each other.

"Even if it was a slave, I'd investigate it," Ashurta said.

"Put it aside for now, and see to Lilliana's safety concerns right away."

"I told you, I'm not partial to it."

"If you won't guard her, I'll have to assign

someone else," Birsha said gruffly.

"I will need all my men for this city. I saw its condition as I rode in. There are many more people than there should be. I saw violence seething below the surface. We were met with great antagonism along the streets we rode in on. Is it that way all over the city?"

Birsha glanced at Lilliana who wrung her hands in consternation. She didn't want to tell this distant cousin of the fight she'd had or any other problems in the city. She thought the temple could influence the city residents more than a force of arms, and she said, "I think the people will bow to the commands of the temple. You needn't trouble yourself with such things. The city isn't as bad as it looks, really."

Birsha's eyebrows shot up, but he said, "Nevertheless, I've called Lord Ashurta to this city for work. I suppose he'll have to do it, now that he's here."

"The other cities of the vale are also hiring us on," Ashurta said as he turned and signaled Daniel where he was still hovering by the door. Ashurta noted that he was holding the chest of the gift from the other king.

Daniel stepped forward, saying, "I'm Lord Daniel, brother to Ashurta. I bear the gift from King Bera of Sodom. He sends it in good will." Daniel balanced the chest down and opened the lid. Golden treasures gleamed in the dim light.

King Birsha stepped backwards a pace, then looked at the floor. "What does King Bera want?"

"He sends his gift in good faith," Daniel

replied with a shrug.

"Nonsense," Birsha spit. "He wants something. No gift is ever free from him."

"Be reasonable, Cousin Birsha," Ashurta soothed. "Cousin Bera is allowed to make a gift between kings. Gold is traditionally given, after all."

Birsha grunted. "Enough talk of our demanding cousin. Come, come, Cousin Daniel, put that chest down and come greet me."

Appearing reluctant, Daniel obeyed. The two men grasped arms and Birsha grinned at the youth's discomfiture. He was apparently unused to matters of state and stepped back awkwardly.

"Take it away," Birsha commanded. "I'm now obligated to reply in kind to King Bera."

A guard rushed up to retrieve the chest of gold.

"Come my cousins, walk with me. I will tell you of our beautiful city."

"I need to see to the animals," Daniel spoke up. "They've walked all night."

"I think I need to get right on the problems, after what I've seen of this city," Ashurta said.

"It's beauty is hidden sometimes, don't be discouraged. Order just needs to be restored."

"Still, I think time is of the essence," Ashurta insisted. "It'll take all my men, and more. Do you have more soldiers?"

King Birsha thought for a moment. "I have the imperial guard, which goes into battle with me. They know the city well. But I'm already stretched thin with protectors. That's why I sent for you, after all."

"I am with Cousin Abraham's group seeking asylum, so it's fortuitous that we can be of service while we are in the Vale of Siddim. The kings have all welcomed us. I thank you for taking us in, Cousin."

"It's my duty," Birsha said. Then he turned to her. "Lilliana, you will need full-time guards from now on."

"I've been thinking," Lilliana decided. "I don't think I'll need a guard, after all." Only until the memory of the death fades as it will in time, she amended to herself. After awhile, she'd be able to go back to doing things the way that she had always done. It would only be a matter of waiting it out.

"Nonsense, Lilliana," the king growled. "You'll have some from my personal guard since Cousin Ashurta here is reluctant. He seems to think his resources are best used in other ways."

"Good," Ashurta sniffed. "I'll need all my men to bring order to this city."

Lilliana resented his tone, and his high-handed manner. To be fair, she was unaccustomed to men in this city speaking down to her because of her elevated position. In theory, she wielded much power, but she'd gotten herself into a dilemma through no fault of her own. She'd had to defend herself, and in truth, she'd been trained at court to defend herself from attacks since she was a young girl. She was, after all, as royal as the king or these cousins from afar.

"The city is really well organized, you just haven't seen it at its best," Birsha said.

Lilliana traced a spiral pattern on the tiles with her foot. "I'm feeling much better about my situation, King Birsha. I'll return to the temple now." Lilliana thought that there was no way that Ashurta could find out that she'd been the one to kill the governor's son, and that the few witnesses had been sufficiently bribed. It really was no worse than any other day in Gomorrah, if she truly looked at it pragmatically. Just because it had happened to her….

She bowed to the king who held out his hand for her to rise, and she kissed his signet ring. "By your leave."

"Until we next meet, go with El," Birsha said.

Ashurta scowled, but turned away from her and stepped closer to the king. He'd dismissed her, and Lilliana thought she didn't want to warrant his attention, if she could help it. He was too confident for his own good. Well, Gomorrah would put him in his place, she would bet on it.

She signaled the two imperial guards that King Birsha assigned to her, and scurried out into the bustling city and made her way back to the temple. She prayed to El as she walked that he'd see her safely throughout the day. She had much to do at the temple.

\*\*\*

Godolfin watched from outside the temple. His man hadn't come back last night. He was one of his biggest supporters and had been financing the rise to power in Gomorrah and in the neighboring cities. But the wealth that had started him on his quest had been stretched thin. The man was supposed to have brought him more riches last night. It had taken some time this morning to learn that his man had hit the temple. The fool, hitting a sacred place, but Godolfin was a prophet and could entreat the god of the city in his own behalf. Today's rebellion had been a small one, and only managed to get the attention of the governor. He needed that money and jewels for the later rebellion that would precede his rise to ultimate power.

It would take entreating the gods again. It was time for another human sacrifice. That would appease his god and put him back in control. He turned to his underling standing next to him as he pushed his long blonde hair out of his face, "Gather everyone at the cave. It is time for another ritual."

"Where will the sacrifice come from?" the underling asked, running his hand over the pommel of his sword.

"Take one from the inner-city and bring it," he ordered.

The ritual would happen tonight while the elites were feasting at the palace. A palace that should rightfully be his. And soon would be, the gods be willing.

\*\*\*

After Lilliana had departed for the temple and Daniel had returned from seeing to the animals, King Birsha sat back in his throne and bid Ashurta and Daniel to approach. "Cousins, let us talk further and start by telling me what has delayed your arrival this morning. I expected you yesterday."

"I have a small army with me and it took time to rally the men. They are still disheartened to have left Shinar but are loyal to the prophet Abraham, our cousin," Ashurta answered. "I didn't know it would be so urgent. Next time tell me in the message of the disorder that it is afoot and I'll come speedily."

When they'd spoken of their families, and exchanged polite news, Birsha said again, "I expected you yesterday. What has delayed you?"

"I apologize, my king. The delay couldn't be avoided. There was unrest in the City of Sodom, and Lot called a council of all his captains and generals."

"What type of unrest?"

"Mobs raiding affluent neighborhoods and gang rapes. I'm afraid Cousin Lot has much to attend to nowadays."

"Are they random crimes?"

"They appear to be drunken hordes, and nothing more. For now that is what we'll assume. But it is a lot for Lot to handle on his own, even so."

"I'm afraid it is growing worse than that here in Gomorrah, for there is conspiring evil afoot. There is civil unrest on top of the usual spate of crimes. I've been challenged to maintain order. But everyday it grows harder. I will confess that I no longer know if I'm up for the challenge. You will see what I mean. I think that if I'm sovereign that I can bring peace back to Gomorrah, once and for all. I need strength in numbers. I am glad that you have arrived. I will add your forces to my own."

"Is it the influx of newcomers from the famine in the outlands that are causing the problems? Or more of the war victims from my homeland?"

"Come, we will talk more of this city's problems that have prompted me to bring you here," Birsha said. "I would embrace my own blood in the pact of cousinhood. We will have a long and fruitful agreement. Are either of you married? No? Then you should marry fine women from Gomorrah. It'll cement our oaths of the blood."

Ashurta said, "but I prefer to marry a Hebrew woman, as would Daniel. I speak for both of us."

"Come, come, you should keep the bloodlines pristine which the nobility of this city would do for you. For us all."

"Pardon me," Daniel said. "But I don't see that you've married yet either. Perhaps you would do well to marry a good Hebrew woman, also."

Birsha scowled. 'I will not trouble you about this today. We will have plenty of time."

"You are a wise king," Ashurta said. "Father Kem sired a great line in you,"

"As in you," Birsha replied in kind. "And you," he addressed Daniel.

Ashurta approached Birsha and the two embraced, to the discomfort of onlookers who shifted about in their anxiousness for their turns with the king. 'We are in agreement."

"Come, walk with me in the garden," Birsha ordered. "I will hear more supplicants after the noonday feast is over. Then tonight we will celebrate more. You will be pleased with the bounty of this city."

They walked into the gardens. Ashurta stopped and looked over a flowering shrub which had buds that hadn't opened yet.

King Birsha smiled widely at him, then rubbed his palms together and then held them out over a shrub. The shrub quivered and then the buds popped open, spraying the air with their sweet scent.

Ashurta applauded. "I see you have the king's magic still in your genes. I'm afraid the magic has left our side of the cousinhood, except for the prophesying."

"Indeed, our line has been careful with the breeding, as the Anuna instructed. We've only wed other royals to keep the blood pure."

"Our bloodlines have crossed many times," Ashurta commented, inspecting the bush with its fuchsia blossoms.

"I can still do many of the things the forefathers did. If only that were all it took to maintain peace in a city."

"The gift of prophecy is still with us, though." Ashurta assured, "You will be impressed with Cousin Abraham. He is even now divining the future for our stay here. He calculates by the stars, too. He knows more about the heavens and its stars than anyone else you'll find. They say an angel taught him."

"It wasn't enough to save you when your cities were sacked. How strong is he?" Birsha asked.

"It is Jehovah that we follow who has led us through the destruction," Daniel answered. "He is our strength."

"If this is true, we should add his worship in the temple. El is failing this city, I'm afraid."

"El is a strong deity, but this one is stronger. I will tell you about Jehovah," Ashurta said. "He is calling the families together. Cousin Abraham is his faithful prophet."

"Where is Abraham?" Birsha inspected a large white lily along the path they walked.

"He is moving out to other parts of the Land of Shem soon but for now he is outside of Sodom. He would take lands for his grazing sheep. He needs space for his followers and their families. Over three hundred of them are specialized generals who escaped Ur's takeover with him. I've brought some of them here for you. He still has twenty-thousand men strong."

"I should extend hospitality to him. There are hills good for grazing around the Salt Sea south of here. There are aqueducts and canals that can water his flocks that flow from the foothills and wells and the River Jordan. And there are crops aplenty to feed his army. Food we aren't short on. We have other problems."

"Your hospitality is gracious," Ashurta thought aloud. "I'm certain he will take you up on it since I'll now be working with you in this decrepit city"

"There is much wisdom and learning here in Gomorrah," Birsha pointed out. "It must be preserved. You will add to your assignment to preserve the wisdom."

"I will abide by our agreement." Ashurta thought for a moment, then asked, "How will you pay us?"

King Birsha sped up. "I'll have the first ingots delivered to you soon."

"There needs to be a place to stay, too."

"You'll stay in the palace. My barracks are full already with my personal contingent. There are other nobles with their own armed forces in this city. You'll need to watch out for them. Various nobles will spare a room for each of your men. They'll stay in the inner-city. The temple is in the outer city, but there are escape tunnels leading into the palace if there is ever a need. The palace is full of tunnels like all palaces. I'll show them to you later."

"I should like a tour of the palace as soon as possible since we'll be staying here," Ashurta agreed.

"I'll need your forces to be on alert at all times."

"How so?" Ashurta put a hand on the king's arm and stopped him. "Is there to be a civil war?"

"Uprisings are predicted. Be prepared." Birsha removed Ashurta's hand. "You'll remember yourself in the company of the city's nobles. Don't offend them with your bold ways."

"I can't have my hands tied when it comes to running this city."

"I'm still running this city."

"For now. I saw one rebellion already on the roadway this morning." Ashurta frowned at the image of it still imprinted on his mind.

"It has been predicted by my spies." Birsha sighed. "There'll be more."

"We're here now, King Birsha. It'll take time to reclaim the city." Ashurta felt the heat of the rising sun intensely.

They walked along in silence for a time, making their way along the winding path and emerging onto a pond with a fountainhead from a canal. It was being powered by a slave pumping the water with a foot mechanism, striding up and down on it. He nodded to them, concentrating on his task.

"I'll show you something else," Birsha offered. Then he stepped up to the water and swirled his hands over it. A swirling eddy formed, and Birsha laughed as the slave panicked. "Resume your work," Birsha commanded him.

"Enough of your magic tricks," Ashurta said.

"Tell me more about this city," Daniel requested.

"I'll do better than, that. I'll show you the view. Over this way."

A flight of stairs surrounded by foliage rose up on the hillock and they climbed it. A view of the high temple opened up. It was stepped with gardens on its ledges. It rose up like a verdant hill in the east end of the city. Ashurta stopped to admire it, and the king doubled back to stand next to him.

"From here, the city looks magnificent,"

Daniel spoke up.

"I want you to bring this city to its knees," King Birsha said.

Ashurta stared at the line of the city and nodded his understanding.

# CHAPTER THREE

Lilliana wound her way through crowd at the market on her way back to the temple with the new guard in tow. She admitted to herself that she felt more confident now that she was being guarded. Yet she hoped that the sudden addition of a guard didn't alert anyone to the reason that she suddenly needed to be guarded.

She shook off the thought, as she bumped into a display cart when avoiding an unaware group of shoppers. The guard righted her, and she cast him a grateful look, but she thought she'd bruised her hip.

She moved on, heading for the cloth merchant she preferred. Stopping off at the cart laden with colorful folds of linen and wool cloth, she looked about for Neanna. Peering into the three-story house behind the cart, Lilliana called out for the merchant woman.

A moment later, Neanna appeared with a

rolling gait, her hands around her protruding belly as if to support her pregnancy. The auburn haired cherubic woman looked gladdened to see Lilliana.

"Greetings, High Priestess," she said with a tentative smile.

"How are you feeling this morning, Neanna?"

"Fair," she said. "I feel that the babe is sitting lower and it could be any day."

"Wonderful news," Lilliana gasped. Pregnancy was a state that she never anticipated experiencing for it went with her office of high priestess to be celibate in deed. Still, she felt the ancient kinship between women of the understanding of the miracle of life-giving. "Who will help you with the birth?"

"Lady Anisha will be my midwife."

Lilliana knew of her. She was a popular healer and midwife. Some of the nobility utilized her, also. "I wish you good fortune with your new babe."

They talked then of the cloth and Neanna's husband's plight as a new slave. "I'm worried about him being taken in slavery. It isn't fair," Neanna said with a frown.

"Perhaps that is a change that should come now," Lilliana stated. "I don't believe in the slavery caste, and think there is a better way of it for the future. I will try again to convince my brother. Perhaps he can have sway over the city assembly. I will propose they put it to the vote."

"Anything would help." Neanna scrunched up her face as if about to cry.

Lilliana wanted to support Neanna in her wares to help their cause. It helped that they were the best cloth in the city. "How is your husband faring with his new enslavement?" She cocked an eyebrow.

"He is most worried that the babe will be born into a slavery household," she answered, rubbing her belly under the golden robe.

"I want to support your products so that he can get out of debt faster, perhaps buy his freedom back."

"Thank you most kindly, High Priestess. It's because of people like you that I'm still a free woman." Her lip quivered. "Won't you buy something again today?"

Lilliana felt warmth suffuse her face as she ordered up several bolts of the refined cloth that she hoped would grow more popular with the city dwellers to help this young couple. But the truth was that there were more vendors competing with Neanna, and to top that the city had taken on an attitude of its fashions being discardable and therefore spent less on them than in the old days. Because Lilliana had been raised in the royal house and taught to expect quality products, she expected she'd patronize Neanna's cart for a long time. But these days, the fashionable young buyers were going to Neanna's competition. She suggested, "Neanna, perhaps you should consider also selling some of the cheap fabric that is the fashion right now."

"I have a family tradition to uphold and vendors that depend upon my buying their wares over the years. I'm beholden."

"But it could make you more money that you need right now. Anyhow, I'll be back for more in a few days. I have several occasions coming up to dress for."

"Check back with me next week as there'll be new cloth from the wool of the newly arrived Hebrews. Their wool is most glorious, I can tell you. It's the quality you're used to, I've seen it already."

"Thank you for telling me. I will do that," Lilliana said sweetly.

A woman approached her from the side. "High priestess Lilliana, how good to see you this morning," the golden haired woman said. Her young pretty face broke into a smile.

Lilliana turned to her. It was the woman who hoped to marry her brother, the king. She smiled at her ambitious friend. "Gracilga how good to see you."

"How is King Birsha today?"

"I've just left him, and he is entertaining our distant cousins. They just arrived."

"Who are they?" Gracilga asked innocently while she fiddled with a bolt of cloth.

"The Hebrews have arrived all the way from Ur in Shinar. They are serious and dour so I expect your help in entertaining them while they are here."

"How long are they staying?"

"I don't know. The king has engaged them to bring this city back to a state of order. King Birsha is taking a drastic step bringing in an outside force. This city runs by its nobles and their armies during regular times, but things have been changeing."

"Not to mention the governor and his army are having to be enforcers."

"Yes, I just saw him this morning handling a slave rebellion." Lilliana shivered at the thought of it and how she'd feared that the governor knew her secret when he'd seen her. Gracilga didn't miss it and looked pointedly at Lilliana's obvious guard.

"You are in some kind of trouble," Gracilga frowned but managed to make it look pretty.

"Why do you say that?" She stepped back a pace. Then she noted the new pendant Gracilga was wearing. "That star pendant, it isn't your right to wear it," Lilliana scolded.

Gracilga put her hand over the long pendant, covering the circle with the star in it. "Tell me about why you have a guard? I heard there was trouble at the temple. You're in trouble again, aren't you?"

Lilliana resented Gracilga's tone and felt frustration and a thread of dread come over her. "Why? What have you heard?"

"I heard there is a dead body that was hidden."

How had she heard so quickly? "Gracilga, you really shouldn't listen to gossip."

"I see by your face that it is true. I knew it. It has something to do with you."

"I can't discuss temple business, you know that," Lilliana said. "My work there is sacred."

"Come, come, I've been your friend for a very long time," she replied.

Neanna moved closer as if to intervene if

needed. Lilliana nodded at the merchant woman. She reassured her with a smile.

"Gracilga, I've known you a long time. You must believe me. There is nothing wrong."

"I heard it was the governor's son."

"I think you shouldn't listen to gossip. You weren't there –"

"I knew it. It's true."

"Let's not talk of it," Lilliana said. "It isn't fitting for conversation."

"I know something else. There is a new prophecy from Godolfin."

Lilliana blanched. That hateful name. "You are listening to more gossip. Nothing good comes from the Order of Godolfin."

"You can doubt after the other prophecies came true?"

"They are evil. That is enough reason to disregard them."

Neeana interjected, "It is true. He is prophecying an end to the kingship. By the new moon."

"Is he trying to incite a rebellion?" Lilliana gasped.

"I wonder if he'll make it so," Gracilga said.

"The king must be notified of this right away. He will have to fortify his army, and get the other nobles to combine their armies with his if this threat of a takeover is serious," Lilliana surmised aloud.

"Let's talk more tonight at the feast." Gracilga touched her pendant again, a dreamy look coming into her eyes. "I hope you'll put in a good word for me with King Birsha." She smiled with anticipated delight.

"Gracilga, I think that you can tout your own praises to him." It was no secret that Gracilga had her sights set on the king. "Is that why you're wearing the royal emblem?"

"I can hope, can't I?" Gracilga turned to Neanna and ordered some of the new cloth arriving soon. Then she turned back to Lilliana.

"I really must be moving along," Lilliana stated.

"I will sit by you at the feast tonight. You can tell me about it later," Gracilga whispered conspiratorially before touching her arm in understanding and moving along.

"Neanna," Lilliana said. "I'll put in a good word with King Birsha. Perhaps he can help your husband." In truth, the king had the power to free slaves, but she couldn't recall the last time that he had done so.

"Thank you, High Priestess. I hope you can convince him to change the slave decree. My husband is a good man. It's not his fault that the debts grew greater than our income. Now it is even more futile because without him working beside me, the debt will remain for the three years."

"You have many new cloths and yours are the most refined in the city. Perhaps you can sell them outside the city, also. To the other cities or travelling merchants."

"I will do what I can," Neanna answered. She rubbed her belly meaningfully.

"That is all one can do. Keep the balance,

and the gods will return you to favor," Lilliana comforted, then paid for her purchase and moved along to the sandal merchant. Her new guard followed a few paces behind, looking alert. She headed for the next wagon stall.

Kilgal, the sandal merchant looked up at her from his short height. He was broad and brawny, but very short and Lilliana smiled down at him. "I'd like to see what you have that is new. I have a feast to attend today and would like something other than this worn out pair, although they are still comfortable. Your workmanship is always superb, after all. But I need something beautiful for tonight."

"Thank you, high priestess. I'm honored by your business."

"What do you have that is festive?"

"I have something special just for you. Wait here." He strode back into his three-story house behind the cart and returned a moment later. "I have these in red or in blue. Or I can make you some that are painted with gold leaf if you give me time."

Fingering the supple leather sandals, Lilliana tested them both before declaring the red ones would do for today. "But I should like a pair of golden ones. Please make those for me."

"I will need some time to make them," he pleaded.

"I will need them for the new moon ceremony. Can you have them by then?"

"What is special about that ceremony, for these will be very special sandals?"

"It's a time for new prophecies coming out.

All will have to heed them," she explained.

Kilgal scowled. "Have you heard the prophecies of the secret prophet, Godolfin?"

Lilliana shivered. There was that name again. She hoped he wouldn't come after her for killing one of his followers. She didn't want to encourage Kilgal in believing in him. "I have not. It isn't wise to heed such a specter of a man. I don't believe he is a prophet."

"Then I won't talk to you of it," he soothed.

Lilliana shivered again. That the Order of Godolfin was gaining more reach was apparent. She needed to keep an eye on her followers. They should be persuaded to stay with the true god of the city. She wondered absently if the new god the Hebrews had brought with them would gain any influence in the city. It was her job to further the worship of El and the rest of the gods and goddesses who covered all aspects of life. This Hebrew god would just have to remain in the background.

Finishing up her transaction for the sandal purchases she told the vendor one more time not to follow Godolfin. For good measure, she gave him a stern look.

She took her new sandals and beckoned the guard. It was time to return to the temple. The reminder about the evil order had soured her morning again. Throwing herself into the temple's work would be a respite.

She moved on, heading back to the temple, the guard a few paces behind her. At the entrance, she turned to him and said, "I'll be fine from here."

He frowned at her dismissal. "You weren't

fine yesterday, High Priestess. I should come inside with you."

He made a point. "Well, try to stay out of the way."

They entered through the huge carved doors, walking into the chamber where the wild lion of the temple roamed. It was tame, but still impressive. A lioness wrapped herself around one of the potted trees. The trees leaned toward the light filtering in from the high windows in the cavernous chamber. Frescoes were painted along the walls of exotic scenes with animals that hadn't all roamed the earth in a long time and lush vegetation from early in Creation.

Lilliana made her way to the inner chambers, and stopped before the holy of holies where she'd do her oblations soon. Today she was working on a hymn to Ishtar, and she needed to have it ready for the feast tonight. If she hadn't been waylaid last night, she would've put the finishing touches on the hymn already. She wound around to her upper chamber and deposited her purchases from the market. Turning to the door, she nodded as the guard took up his watchful stance.

"What is your name?" she asked.

He looked at her. "I'm called Algarit."

"Algarit. Thank you for guarding me. I'm afraid there won't be anything interesting today."

"I don't require entertainment, High Priestess."

Lilliana smiled a small smile, then closed the door and took up a seat at the table.

She pulled out the papyrus with the hymn

and began to sing.

*****

The feast proceeded with merriment. The long low tables arranged around the chamber held the nobles of the city and the royal relatives and a few friends of the king. Ashurta surveyed the scene and found the high priestess at the head of one table with another beautiful woman. They were engaged in a conversation. The whole chamber buzzed with the various conversations and in one corner of the room a musical group played their pipes and drums while a songstress warbled.

He had heard gossip while he investigated the murder of the governor's son. Rumors that placed Lilliana there. He'd paid handsomely for the information but the payments had come out of the city's coffers. He'd handled the poor before in Ur and so the witnesses had been forthcoming with the information. He had the king's permission to conduct his business in the city any way he saw clear to do it. Staring hard at Lilliana and catching her eye, he scowled and she looked away.

Rising from his silk cushioned seat, he pulled at his fine robe to put it back in place. Underneath he was garbed in his armor still, ever ready. Then he walked up to her and tapped her on the shoulder.

She turned and peered up at him. "Yes, Lord Ashurta?"

"We need to talk." He attempted a friendly smile but failed at it.

"Now?"

He nodded solemnly, then held out a hand to help lift her up. She placed her elegant hand in his and he sucked in his breath at the sudden closeness as she stood next to him. He'd thought her beautiful from the first glance, but in her festive raiment she was more radiant than he remembered.

He mentally shook off the feeling. "Come with me."

He still held her hand and tugged her along between the tables until they were outside on a patio lined by standing pillars carved with more mystical animals. She extracted her hand from his and rubbed it where he'd been holding it too tightly as though he wasn't sure she wouldn't come along.

"What is so urgent that it can't wait until the hours of court?" she asked, pushing an errant lock of dark hair back. Her hazel eyes glowed with energy and something else he couldn't place.

"Why didn't you tell me you killed the governor's son?" he asked.

"How … How did you find out?" Her lower lip trembled and she blinked back suddenly moist eyes.

"Did you think that I wouldn't? I spent all day, time wasted if you'd only told me right away instead of leaving me to make a fool of myself in front of the city."

She turned her fine head away, staring at the dark garden. "The witnesses were sworn to secrecy."

"That's the trouble with paying them off. For a few bags of barley more, they can all be convinced to talk."

"Which they did?"

"They did. It wasn't hard to get the facts from them after the first one turned. Now tell me, why did you lie to me?"

"I didn't lie, exactly. I just withheld the truth. Surely you can understand my position?"

"I have much to do in this city," Ashurta said gruffly. "Your cooperation would've been best."

She looked him straight in the eye and pulled herself up to her full height. "I didn't think anyone should know about it."

"It's too late. The whole city likely knows by now. Once a secret is out, the penalty is bound to follow."

She exhaled a heavy sigh. "I'm in danger now."

"You have a guard with you at all times from now on." Ashurta felt frustration arise. King Birsha had been right, this woman was in need of guarding at all times.

"I do. I won't go anywhere without one."

"You don't have a choice in the matter." His tone brooked no argument.

"I had hoped it'd be otherwise."

"Are you safe at the temple now?" he asked.

"There are temple guards."

"But the assassin got in once before. There could be more bent on revenge, or to finish what the first one failed to do."

She winced at his words. "I have to live at the temple."

"You can move into the palace for awhile," he said, not unkindly. He was already enjoying the temple amenities, himself.

A breeze lifted an errant lock of her hair, and he watched it with fascination.

"I can't forsake the temple. It is my duty to be there."

"Then I will verify the fortifications myself. I may not approve of your methods, but I'll make sure that you're safe." Despite her allure, he did disapprove, and folded his arms.

"I can't have my work there interrupted," she said sternly.

"It is imperative that I do this, and I require your cooperation."

"Alright. I'll cooperate. But I don't want the people hindered from seeking me out at the temple. It is my sacred duty to be there for them." She pushed back the loose lock of her hair.

"I will respect that, but I also have a duty, and that includes ensuring your safety."

"Maybe this will all go back to normal soon." She looked worried.

"I wouldn't count on that. Stay alert." He was done scolding her.

She stared up at him with those luminous eyes, and he felt the ice around his heart melting. He wondered about it because as a high priestess she was off limits. His heart would have to look elsewhere. Besides, he'd thought her a pampered woman of his own royal class, something he disrespected. But her dedication to her work was convincing him otherwise. Or perhaps he was simply falling for her beauty, something he should guard against.

Turning away from him, she cast a glance over her shoulder as she asked, "are we done?"

"I think I've made things clear enough."

Her chin dropped as she nodded, then she pivoted on her heel and walked back to the feast. He watched her rigid back as she walked away from him. He stood there alone for a few more minutes before rejoining the king.

*** 

"What was that handsome man interested in you about?" Gracilga prodded as Lilliana resumed her seat.

Lilliana pushed back her sleeves and reached for a piece of bread and dipped it in olive oil. It's herbs flared her senses as she took a bite. Sipping at her fig wine, she looked back at Gracilga's expectant face.

"Well?" Gracilga prompted.

Lilliana chewed thoughtfully. "It has to do with the crimes in the city." She didn't feel like talking about it.

"I knew it. You're involved. I told you I'd heard the rumors," Gracilga said.

"I am trying to remain uninvolved. The temple is my focus."

"But something happened, didn't it? In the temple, I mean."

"I'm not in any trouble if that's what you're worried about," Lilliana replied.

"I heard you killed a man. It's true, isn't it?"

"I had to defend myself. Now you know. Don't tell anyone. Besides, where did you hear it at?"

"Rumors around the marketplace. People talking. Gossip." Gracilga shrugged. "You know the kind."

"I'm not usually involved in any kind of gossip." Lilliana sipped at her wine. "I live a simple clean life at the temple. I treat the people well, and the city supports me."

"I think you're too cut off there from the real world. You don't know what is going on right under your very nose in this city. You don't interact with the people the way you should to know what is happening in their lives. You're isolated." Gracilga reached for her own bronze goblet.

"I don't know how you could say that. I'm involved with the people every day. I know what they need. Any of them can come to the temple for meals during the day. You're wrong about it."

"I don't think I'm wrong. I think you used to be in touch with the commoners, but not anymore. When's the last time you went to one of the commoners' houses to see how they live? The poor are getting poorer all the time. The number of slaves is increasing, and children have to work instead of going to school. You're so surrounded by your palace walls or the temple that you are no longer are in touch with the real people and their problems, which are increasing."

Lilliana gasped. "I can't believe that you're saying this to me, Gracilga."

"Think about it. You're in trouble in many ways. The city is about to rise up and you don't have a clue."

"More of your rumors?"

Gracilga coughed delicately into her palm. "You're out of touch."

"That's harsh, and I don't believe the city will revolt. Those are rumors that have been around a long time. Nothing has happened yet."

"The city has gotten evil and debase. Like the sister cities. Especially Sodom no longer allows one basic human dignity. You couldn't get me to go to that city if my life depended upon it."

"I'm just concerned with Gomorrah. It is my whole focus to be an intermediary between the gods and the people." Lilliana picked up a grape and popped it into her mouth, then turned to face Gracilga squarely. "I'm not out of touch."

"You are. Just watch more closely and you'll see what I mean. I am going to get myself a guard, too. The streets are that dangerous now. You should know that, but you don't." Gracilga pouted prettily.

Lilliana glared at her, feeling ire at her friend's attitude that she hadn't felt before. But then she'd never killed a man before. Things were changing quickly. What if Gracilga was right?

"Perhaps you should introduce me to your new friend," Gracilga changed the subject. "That handsome man. He could be my guard anytime."

Lilliana speared a piece of lamb with a skewer, and bit. She chewed thoughtfully. "Perhaps. He is my distant cousin. A Hebrew. I don't know what he is doing here in the city except that he had to leave Ur. King Birsha has him doing something."

"A Hebrew, huh?" Gracilga asked. "I expect their fine wool will take over the city. I heard about it already at the marketplace."

"He follows a prophet-king named Abraham, another of my royal cousins. They brought many sheep and soldiers. Abraham say there'll be a famine soon. He has been prophesying. He says that death and destruction will come upon the cities of the vale if they don't repent."

"Repent?" Gracilga looked incredulous. "Placating the gods I should think would preserve this city, although it's about to rise up."

"And he says angels told him to prophesy it."

"Is he a crazy visionary man?"

"He is a leader from Ur. Of royal blood." Lilliana turned back to her meal. "We have to listen to him, but I don't see how we can follow his orders. The people won't listen to a stranger, although they might listen to me and the high priest."

"Then this Abraham is probably useless except for his wool."

Lilliana pouted. "A thousand of his soldiers have moved into the city today. They're led by Lord Ashurta. That man you asked about."

Gracilga continued, "I, for one, might be inclined to believe Abraham after all. I think this city has gotten too wicked. Every day there are worse crimes. Criminals are taking over the neighborhoods. There are so many private armies. I suspect that there'll be battles soon within the city."

"I've heard whispers of revolution from temple goers, but I don't know if they're true," Lilliana said.

"You would know more about it than I, with your position at the temple."

"I should discuss this with King Birsha," Lilliana decided.

"What are you going to tell him?"

"That there are rumors."

"When are you going to tell him, since you haven't told him by now?"

"There's no good time to do it so I'll go do it now. Wait here. You'll be fine until I return."

"I want to hear this." Gracilga looked at her with a glowing smile. "I want to come with you. I want to talk to the king, too."

"You're incorrigible, Gracilga. This fascination you have with the king isn't going anywhere."

"I can hope," Gracilga whispered.

"Alright. Come with me." Lilliana softened. She hadn't talked to her brother since the morning when she'd admitted her dilemma so she didn't know what had transpired afterward with the Hebrew cousins, but there had been Hebrew soldiers at the temple already talking of Abraham. She glanced across the room at the king and her cousins all sitting together.

The two women made their way around the arranged low tables full of feasters to the king's table. Ashurta sat to Birsha's right, and Daniel to Ashurta's right, and the governor on the king's left.

The ladies held hands as they approached. They knelt beside them and the two men turned to see them.

"What is it, Lilliana?" King Birsha asked. He took her hand and squeezed it reassuringly.

Ashurta eyed her with suspicion, but then smiled. Daniel looked around him. The governor nodded to her, then turned back to the man on his left.

"Gracilga and I were just discussing Gomorrah and the new prophecy of its demise," Lilliana said.

"There's more than one prophecy going around." The king cleared his throat. "Ashurta, do you hold to Abraham's new prophecy?" Birsha asked.

"King Birsha, I have to follow Abraham. My first loyalty is to him," Ashurta said.

"What is this new prophecy?" Lilliana asked.

"Ashurta, tell her. She needs to prepare," Daniel said.

"High Priestess, it is that there will be a famine in the land. It will go on for a long time."

"I don't believe it," Lilliana said.

"We have so much rain," Gracilga piped in.

"Nevertheless," Birsha said. "Cousin Abraham is a prophet and he would only tell us the truth. He was a great man in Ur, after all."

"He is my spiritual leader, and now you are my secular leader," Ashurta said. "I feel his prophecies have come about in the past, in one form or another."

"The prophecy says that the Vale of Siddim will face famine soon, doesn't it?" Birsha asked.

"It is true that that is the prophecy. It is time for the cities to put up food stores against the famine." Daniel reached for his goblet and took a swig. "There is still time."

"How much do you believe this prophecy?" Gracilga leaned toward the king.

"I, for one, would listen to it." Lilliana said.

"I want to know more about it; how much time do we have?" Gracilga asked.

"How much time do we have?" King Birsha echoed.

"I think that Jehovah is giving the people as much warning as possible," Ashurta said. "But the cities should act now."

"Well, I for one think that something can be done," Lilliana said. "The temple can initiate the food storage plans. The people will have to follow our instructions." She shifted in her kneeling position uncomfortably.

"Ashurta is beginning the clamp down on the city now. There should be good changes soon from it," Birsha said thoughtfully. "The people will become obedient again, you'll see."

"I can't believe this great city with all its wisdom and learning can't be saved," Gracilga said.

"Well, thank you for the warning, Cousin Ashurta," Lilliana said begrudgingly. "What else do you have for this city?"

"I was just talking to the king about the fact that an army is approaching."

King Birsha frowned. "I think we are safe

on that account because we pay our tribute to King Chedorlaomer. He's here to collect it and protect us. I didn't have time to tell you that, Ashurta and Daniel, before these ladies approached."

"That may be true enough, but we don't know how the army will behave when it's here," Ashurta said.

"You've lived through your home city being destroyed before in Ur. I see that that is why you are nervous about an army."

"Ur was an uprising. I'm also alert to that here," Ashurta said.

"Tell me, was there a prophecy for that one too?" Birsha asked.

Ashurta rubbed his chin. "There was one. But I doubted it, at first. And yet it came true."

"Well, I don't think that another army can overcome this city, or all of the other cities combined." Birsha said. "That is, if it came down to that."

"But King Chedarloamer conquered this area once before," Daniel said.

"I will do my best to move this city into righteousness. Then Jehovah will be on our side. That should solve the problem," Ashurta said with conviction.

Gracilga looked doubtful. "I heard of another prophecy, one that the citizens believe."

Birsha peered at her through squinted eyes. "What is this?"

Gracilga blushed under his attention. "What it is is a prophecy from the underworld of Gomorrah. It is affecting the citizenry. There's another prophet in the city, one who promises to free the slaves, but he says he'll conquer the city by another full moon."

"Ridiculous," Ashurta said. "This city can't be conquered. For one thing my army is here now. A thousand men strong."

"For another," Birsha added. "The Elamites are protecting us. Besides, the people aren't unhappy with my rule. Why would they rebel?"

"There's something else you should know about this new prophet," Gracilga said.

"I'm not interested in this false prophet," Birsha said.

Lilliana piped in, "Let Gracilga tell us about him. It might be important."

Gracilga gave her a thankful look. "You should know that he demands human sacrifices."

"What?" Ashurta reddened.

"That's outrageous," Birsha exclaimed.

"There's more to it," Gracilga added. "He claims to be a royal and claims the throne."

"How do you know all this, Gracilga?" Lilliana watched her friend closely.

"I am not out of touch with the people like you are." She plaited the edge of her robe with nervous fingers. "I am one of the common people, after all." She gave Birsha a longing look that even he noticed.

"I see," Birsha said. "That you wear the symbol of this court. The pentacle. Is that because you're with us, or are you sympathetic to this … this false prophet?"

"His name is Godolfin, and no one knows

where he hides," Gracilga avoided answering the question but she fingered the pentacle necklace.

"What is it?" Ashurta asked. "Where do your loyalties lie?"

"I am faithful to this crown. To King Birsha." Her face remained solemn.

"See that you don't go spreading more about this false … Godolfin than necessary." Birsha clenched his fists. "You don't want to create a fascination about him with the other commoners. They have enough to focus on with the renewed demands that they abide by the laws of the city."

"I won't," Gracilga said in a small voice. "I hope I haven't upset you." She looked at the king. Her pupils flared.

"Not enough to evict you." Birsha frowned. "It seems you are just carrying rumors. See that you carry them no further."

"Still," Lilliana said. "We can't ignore that there is a deadline of the next new moon. It could start an uprising if the people believe Godolfin."

"Ashurta will flush out this false prophet and his minions, won't you?" Birsha asked.

"As you command," he stated as he signaled a serving girl for more fig wine. He resumed, "Take care, ladies, that you don't fall prey to this new prophet rising up in the city. He will have to be put down once and for all and I don't want you caught up in the fall."

The serving girl refilled their wine and gave goblets to the ladies. They all drank together in a solemn silence. Lilliana wondered if there was anything else happening in the city that she should know about. Perhaps she was out of touch.

# CHAPTER FOUR

Ashurta felt warmth from the food and wine suffusing him when King Birsha turned to him and said, "The prophecies disturb me. I'm afraid they'll cause the city to rise up."

"I had thought of that, too," Ashurta agreed.

The king's knuckles showed white as he grasped his goblet. "I am going to dispatch spies about the city. New ones. The ones I have didn't bring me the news, instead it was a love-besotted follower who did. I don't like it."

"Gracilga might be mistaken about it. She is imbibing after all," Daniel suggested.

"True. There's more to it," Birsha said. "She'd do about anything to get my attention."

"She is a lovely woman. Why don't you consider her?" Ashurta had to ask.

"She is too innocent if you can believe that anyone in this city could be innocent," Birsha answered.

"I don't know. She seems worldly enough to me," Daniel said, picking up a bite of lamb.

"You must be used to different kinds of women. When I take my pleasure, I like more worldly women. But enough of this talk. I want you to send out spies into the city from your soldiers."

"I will need all the soldiers to bring order to this city." Ashurta scowled. "I don't think I can spare any. Besides, wouldn't your imperial guards be better at the job? They already know the city."

The king shook his head. "You will have to spare a league of them for this. I will supply you the missing soldiers from my own private force."

"Very well." Ashurta expelled a harsh breath. "I will dispatch soldiers tonight to do the spying."

"We will hear back from them every day, no matter what." Birsha stood then, to make his rounds of the banquet.

"I should like to do the spying," Daniel said with a grin.

"Right," Ashurta said.

"Be diligent," Birsha said.

"I will," Daniel said.

"Then I will leave you now to go about it." Ashurta rose also and bowed to the king. He cast a glance toward Lilliana at one corner of the table before heading out into the night to communicate with his army. His work was just beginning in the city of Gomorrah.

***

Lilliana wended her way home to the temple after the banquet. Her guard was a few paces behind her when she heard him suddenly draw his sword. Her heart stuttered.

Shadows moved quickly and suddenly they were engaged in battle.

She reached for her knife and brandished it. The guard engaged the unexpected assailants with his sword.

"Get behind me," the guard commanded.

But she could fight, too, and so she struck at one of the two attackers.

The swords of the guard and the other attacker clashed.

Lilliana used her large knife to parry the other attacker but he was stronger than her, and she fell to the ground. She rolled away faster than he could reach her and she was on her feet again.

The moonlight glinted off of the weapons as she fought back with all her might.

The dark hid their faces, and she wondered if she knew them. She saw so many citizens from the temple. Did she know who was trying to kill her? Why were they attacking?

"What do you want?" she yelled.

Under the moonlight, she saw her attacker smile in an imitation of a snarl.

The guard reached for her and pulled her behind him. "Run," he said.

He was engaging the two swordsmen now, and Lilliana felt his urgency as he shoved her away behind him.

"Run!"

She did as he said, and her legs carried her swiftly back to the palace. She bypassed many curious eyes along the way, glowing in the dark under the moonlight as people stepped back to let her pass. At the entrance to the palace, she slid to a stop and banquet attendees parted for her where they stood.

"Help, help!" she shouted.

Guards came rushing out and surrounded her. She told them of the attack.

Daniel rushed past others and grasped Lilliana by her elbow. "What happened to you?"

"My guard and I were just attacked, by the marketplace. I came back to get help."

"Then we must hurry," Daniel said as his hand landed on his sword. He clacked it. "Guards, come with us. Lilliana, show us the way."

"Daniel, Lilliana," Ashurta yelled out as he pushed through the throng of people at the entrance to stop at their side. "What is it?"

"Lilliana was attacked on the way to the temple," Daniel said.

"Let's go," Ashurta barked.

She turned and ran again toward where she'd left the guard doing battle. The moon lit up the roadway and showed a crowd of people gathered around where the fight was.

The crowd parted and she came upon the fallen body of her personal guard.

She screamed.

\*\*\*

Ashurta surveyed the scene. Lilliana was huddled by the body of the guard that gave his life to save her. This attack couldn't have been random because Lilliana was known city-wide. She was famous among all the people, arguably as powerful as the king. Only the governor wielded more power.

The bloodied corpse was being lifted now to be carried away with as much dignity as his men could give it on a liter. His sword and parts of his armor was missing, whether from the assailants or by the people of the city watching he didn't know. It was shameful.

Lilliana stood upright and brushed back her tousled dark hair. In the dim light, he could see tears marring her face. He approached her.

"What kinds of weapons were they using?"

"Swords," she choked out.

He reached out a comforting hand to her shoulder. She turned to face him.

"I think this is the retaliation. I've never been attacked before," she offered.

"Except at the temple, you said. When you had to kill."

"Yes. There."

"That may be the motivation. Or it could also be simple robbery. You're wearing a lot of lapis lazuli, after all."

She reached up to her layered necklaces. "I've always worn these and other jewels."

"Times must be worsening in the city."

"It could be greed, but I suspect that it's the retaliation," she cried. "Maybe the city is growing worse."

"I saw the city on my patrols today. What I saw was a lot of petty crime on the streets. Where there's that, there's bound to be worse."

She looked askance. "I need to get home now."

"I'll walk you home," he decided. "From now on, you'll have two of my soldiers with you. King Birsha was right, you need the best I have to offer."

She sighed. "I want to get back now."

Ashurta signaled another soldier and the three set off for the temple.

They wound along the dark streets to the gigantic building that comprised much of the activity of the city. It reminded him of the temple in Ur with it's stepped sides. Unlike the one in Ur, this one had foliage growing on the steppes in an array of gardens. The scent of flowers reached him as they drew close.

"I'll check the temple for you before you go in," he offered.

Lilliana nodded, and then rubbed her arms with her hands. "I'll wait here."

The other guard stepped up beside her, his sword drawn, to wait.

Ashurta entered the temple and was overcome by the artwork on the walls. It was glorious even in the dim light from the torches. Scenes of jungles on one side and an Egyptian plain on the other. He recognized some of the painted animals, but others were mythical or hadn't lived on the planet for a very long time.

A low roar greeted him as he walked further.

A lioness came slinking out of the darkness. This one would be tame, living in the temple as it was. He held out his hand as she approached to sniff him. She butted his hand and he rubbed her head. Another low growl.

He moved on through the long chamber towards the holy of holies. It was curtained off, but since it was a perfect place for an assailant to hide, he parted the curtains and looked up at the statue of El. A muscular bearded diety on an elaborate throne carved out of stone. No one in there.

He walked further around the corner to climb the stairs to the sleeping chambers. He knew Lilliana lived in one and the high priest in the other one. He pulled a torch from the stairwell. He found and inspected her chamber first.

Her elaborately carved furniture and silk cushions and fine wool blankets caught his attention. She lived in as much luxury as if she was in the palace. All about the room, bronze figurines gleamed in the torch light.

Then he moved to the high priest's chamber and rapped on the doorway.

The high priest wasn't back yet from the feast, so Ashurta entered and quickly inspected the apartment. It was similar to Lilliana's chamber.

Satisfied, he made his way to the other rooms of the temple and inspected the kitchen. He counted all the knives hanging from their rack. None seemed to be missing.

He then went to the accounting area. Nothing moved.

He saw through a slit window that the moon

was reaching its apex.

Turning about, he decided it was safe for Lilliana to return to her home. He made his way back to the entrance and told her.

"Thank you," she said gratefully, reaching her hand out to his forearm to squeeze it.

"I'll take the first watch with this guard, and then you'll have two guards with you at all times." Ashurta vowed to Jehovah to keep Lilliana safe, and buoyed himself up to remain awake all night patrolling the temple.

"What is it?" Lilliana peered curiously at him.

"Where are the temple guards?" Ashurta realized with a jolt that he hadn't seen any.

"There are only two at a time, and they can leave for errands."

"The high priest is gone, too. Only the lion seems to be here."

"If the high priest is gone, then that must be where the guards are. Now that I have a guard, he may've felt the need to have one, too. Let's assume that is the case," Lilliana said.

"Then one or both guards may be with the high priest still at the palace." Ashurta noted the moon's glow falling softly on Lilliana where she stood in the doorway of the temple. His heart skipped a beat. His impression of her was changing as he got to know her. She was thoughtful and dedicated and he thought she had inner wells of strength.

He scanned the courtyard behind her and she cleared her throat.

"It's late and the feast will have broken up by now, or soon will," she sighed.

"It requires an explanation, and I'll get one when they return." Ashurta wanted to take control of the temple's defenses right away. He couldn't do half a job, after all. He was committed now to protect his royal cousin and he'd risk his life if he needed to in order to do it.

"Really, the people of Gomorrah have respected this temple all along," she explained.

"Until your problem with the attacker."

"I think we'll have to hire more guards. It hasn't been an issue before," Lilliana said.

"We'll take care of this in the morning. You should get some sleep," Ashurta soothed.

He walked her to her chamber and pulled open the door. Before she passed through, she looked up at him. Then she stood on her toes and planted a kiss on his cheek. He felt her warm breath fan his lips.

"Thank you," she whispered.

Raising an eyebrow, he said, "But High Priestess, I thought you had to be celibate."

The soft look on her face was replaced by a smirk. "It's just a kiss."

He'd assumed too much, she was saying, and he nodded. Her perfume assailed his nostrils and he grudgingly said, "I'll be right outside the door all night.

She nodded and passed inside. He rested a hand on the pommel of his sword, then withdrew it to test its ease in leaving the scabbard. She'd taken him by surprise, that was all. But tonight he'd be alert to any harm. No one would get into the temple except for the high priest and the guards until morning. By his life.

\*\*\*

The flaming cauldron flared inside the echoing cave. The gathered crowd shuffled anxiously. The hooded dark-robed figure of Godolfin stood at the altar where he raised up a crying babe, holding it by the neck. He carried it to the altar, and laid the weakened infant down, holding it prone as he impaled it with the ceremonial implement. The wailing screech erupted into the pregnant silence, but soon quieted down, leaving the cave in silence.

From behind the man-sized gong behind the altar, a giant of a man emerged, his naked body oiled and rippling in the firelight. Except for the weapons strapped to him.

The giant man strode to the center and took the dagger out of its scabbard. He approached the sacrifice, and began his evil ministration. The cloaked figure closest to him walked over with a bronze carved chalice inset with jewels that glittered in the firelight.

With a cut, the giant man drained some of the infant's blood into the chalice, then turned to the audience, and handed the chalice to Godolfin who took a bloody swig.

"Who will join me this day?" Godolfin shouted.

A rousing cry went up from the audience,

echoing in the chamber.

"All hail to Godolfin," the audience chanted.

The frenzy was interrupted when the naked priest hit a gong. The resounding tones silenced the shouts. Godolfin pushed back his hood and sweat gleamed on his features.

"Who will take this blessed corpse for their home this day?" Godolfin called out.

A hunched man approached with a clay jar big enough to fit the sacrifice into. "I will accept the blessing this day."

"Hide it well, and the angel of abundance will find you." He watched the face of the man for signs of doubt, or worse.

"It will be in the appointed spot," the elderly man said.

"You bring abundance for all with it.

A rousing cheer went up as Godolfin inserted the sacrifice into the jar.

Then the man sealed it with a fitted cork.

A woman from the audience rushed forward. "Let me take it. I will place one under my floorboards today."

"Bring me the next sacrifice, and then you may." Godolfin smiled upon her with tolerance.

"Is there nothing I can do until then?" She swiped at a tear.

"Be diligent in the sacrifices to the Great One. Abundance will come to you all for this," Godolfin promised. He withdrew his decorated sword from its scabbard and slashed it ceremoniously through the air. "Join me in praises to the gods."

From behind him, a harp began to strum out a dark hymn. A woman playing it sang in a contralto voice and the chamber quieted. She sang of the creation of man by the gods and the song ended with a stanza of ethereal chords.

A raging chant went up again. It echoed off the cavern walls.

When the chant died down, Godolfin shouted, "Soon we will take Gomorrah, then all of the Vale of Siddim. Then all of the Land of Shem. It's our destiny."

"Hail Godolfin!"

"I will free you from the tyranny of the crown and you shall have your freedom. No more slavery or indenturetude. The rich will no longer rule the cities. Your debts will be forgiven when I rule."

A ripple ran through the robed crowd. Hoods fell back as the attendees jumped and shouted in jubilation.

Godolfin thrust his arm upward and the crowd hushed. "Bring me the coffers of the city, and capture the tribute. I require them." Then he turned to leave.

The obedient crowd fell to their knees, their instructions understood. Godolfin would bring them all power and their hearts desires.

A voice cried out, "Show us more, oh great one!"

While they were bowed in obedience, he lifted the ceremonial dagger and levitated it in the air above the altar. A further hush enveloped the cave, and Godolfin spread his arms wide.

"Follow me where I lead," he said. "I'm your rightful leader."

A murmur ran through the crowd and Godolfin waved to them to rise up. "Begin now to take over the city with our rightful ways. You will be rewarded."

A jubilant shout went up.

Godolfin shouted his pleasure at their obeisance. Then he turned and left.

*** 

Lilliana eased her feast attire off and removed her lapis jewelry for the night. What had she been thinking to give Ashurta a kiss? And he'd taken it wrong, too. It was simple, she found him attractive and wasn't averse to exploring her feelings. Granted, tonight wasn't right.

Her emotions were heightened by the danger she'd faced. She searched her body for bruises and found some forming where she'd been pushed to the ground. Purple welts were on her shoulder and hip where she'd fallen. Locating a bottle of oil she rubbed it on her bruises, then she worked on getting ready for bed.

She'd applied cosmetics so she removed them with another scented oil, then wiped down the rest of her body. Suffused with the sweetness, she slipped into her bed and pulled the silk cover over her head. She surprised herself by drifting off to sleep quickly despite the fear of the day.

When she awoke, the sunlight was coming through the slit windows and landing on her bed.

She'd overslept. Easing out of bed, she stretched like a cat and rubbed her sore side gingerly. Wondering if there was a chance that Ashurta was still outside her door, she pulled on a flowing robe of purple linen and wool and stepped over to the door. She eased it open and saw a strange soldier standing there. By his uniform, she knew he was one of the Hebrew soldiers. Disappointed that it wasn't Ashurta, she nodded to the guard in acknowledgement, and closed the door, wondering how long Ashurta had stayed by her side last night.

Lilliana finished getting ready, applying the imported Egyptian cosmetics quickly and then checking her reflection in the polished copper mirror. She felt a tight knot in her center as she thought more about the attack last night. It was worrisome, and she wanted to talk to the king about it. Determined, she opened the door and told the guard she intended to go to the palace.

He was affable and cheerful, despite what looked like a permanent scowl. They met up with the other guard at the entrance to the temple. Lilliana ignored the arriving throng and pushed through at a quick pace heading toward the palace. She'd find her brother there receiving the supplicants for the day as he usually did. She needed to see him urgently.

\*\*\*

Ashurta watched a bereft woman approach the dais where the king sat on his throne. His audience was in full play when her turn came to approach the throne. She fell to her knees, and clasped her hands to her forehead in evident grief.

"My babe has been taken," the woman in white and gold raiment cried out to King Birsha.

"Tell me what happened, fine lady," King Birsha implored, his scepter punctuating the air.

Beside him, Ashurta stepped forward. "I'll find your babe for you."

She looked up at him with distrust, then looked at the king. "I need help. My baby is gone. Please, you must help me."

"I assign you this woman's plight," Birsha ordered Ashurta. "This isn't the first babe to be taken before. It is a curse in this city."

Ashurta nodded gravely, disturbed. "Tell me about it," he said as he stepped up to the bereaved mother. He lifted her up and led her away to a carved stone bench. She walked on wobbly legs, then sat where he indicated. "What has happened?" he asked as they sat. He signaled one of the scribes to join them.

The scribe rushed across the great hall and settled down with papyrus and red ink, squatting by the other nearby bench where he set down the papyrus and ink. "I'm ready." He bagan to write.

"What happened?" Ashurta prompted, taking her shaking hands in his big ones.

"I … I awoke this morning to silence. Usually the babe coos and gurgles first thing in the morning. She's a very happy baby." She began to cry in earnest.

"Go on," Ashurta felt his heart tighten as he encouraged her.

"I … couldn't find her." She sniffled, and pulled her hands away to wipe the tears away.

"Where did you look?"

"Everywhere in the house and the garden."

Ashurta hadn't heard of infants being kidnapped for a long time, and in the past it had been for a ransom from wealthy families. The more powerful families in Ur had been in danger to such crimes, but he'd just arrived here and judging by this lady's garment she was of the wealthy class. It must be a kidnapping for ransom, then. "Could she have crawled away?"

"No, she isn't old enough to crawl yet. She's just a tiny babe still."

"Tell me what you did."

She sniffed and gathered her courage. "I checked all the windows and one was broken. My husband is gone. He's a successful merchant and is travelling. I didn't know what to do, so I came here."

"Tell me your names, and the babe's name."

"Miriam, and my baby is Este.

Ashurta nodded to the scribe. "Record her address and the time of day she made the discovery."

The scribe asked, "What is your address?"

She rattled off a street name and house description. Ashurta recognized it was in the inner-city. He frowned. The inner-city gate was guarded at night and locked from sundown until sunrise. "Did you have any guests last night? Anyone staying the night?"

"While my husband was gone? Not last

night."

"Miriam, I will search for your babe now. You may still be in danger, yourself. Do you have somewhere you can stay until your husband returns?"

"I don't think so."

"Then I will assign you a guard, and we'll go now to your house and begin the investigation."

"Thank you. Thank you." She grasped Ashurta's forearm, and his muscles flexed under her clutch. "Please find her. You just have to."

Ashurta took a contingent of his soldiers with them to her house so that they could begin the investigation. Miriam led them through the door of her three-story brick house. The brickwork was finely worked to fit together, and the interior of the house was cool despite the rising heat of the day. The tiled entry led into the main room with a dining area at one end and a wall dividing it from the kitchen area. The floor was covered with wooden planks that had been rubbed to a smooth sheen.

Miriam removed her sandals at the door and Ashurta noticed that her toenails were colored. Ashurta and his men left their weapons at the door. She led them into the dining area where they all took seats around the long wooden table.

A slave girl emerged from the shadows and Ashurta noticed that she was shapely and adorned in a white and gold sheath like her mistress. A household signature, he decided. This was obviously a wealthy merchant's home, judging by the size of the house, and the sumptuous fabrics about. The slave girl was also a beauty as could be afforded by the wealthy. She brought a flask and baskets of bread to the table and poured them all wine to drink.

"Join me for breaking the fast first," Miriam said. She stood by the table and waved at it with her hand indicating they should sit.

Ashurta decided he'd ask her more questions as his stomach grumbled in anticipation of the hot bread. The slave girl brought honey to the table and Ashurta nodded to his two soldiers. They all sat around the table and broke the bread between them.

Ashurta talked to Miriam more about the disappearance but while she could tell him all her activities the night before and what time each had occurred, she didn't think she'd heard a sound at any time.

Ashurta then established that two guards would stay with her at all times. "Until the babe is located," he stated. "If you get a ransom note, don't try to respond to it yourself. Call upon me first, understood?"

"I haven't received a demand for ransom yet. Do you think that is all that is wanted? I've heard of other babies disappearing and never being found again." She worried the edge of her gown and tears welled in her eyes.

"I promise you that I'll find your baby if it's the last thing I do," Ashurta promised. His heart clenched at the dread and fear on Miriam's face.

"I'll show you the upstairs room now," she said and on the way stopped at the second floor to show the broken window. A large tree was growing next to it.

"The culprit must've scaled the tree to climb in," Ashurta surmised.

They proceeded to the third floor up the wooden steps. It was a fine house with exotic silk drapings on the walls in bold colors. The hall at the top of the stairwell was lined with slender tables displaying wrought metal sculptures of fantastical animals. One looked like it was of gold.

The bedroom was also lined in the silks and the windows were draped in them to keep out the heat.

"She was over here," Miriam pointed to a wooden cradle at one corner of the bedroom.

The cradle was designed from cedarwood and carved with mythical beasts. It was across from the bed in the room. It held soft woolen and silk wrappings.

"There is no blood that I can see," Ashurta said.

"It was just empty when I awoke," Miriam said with a fresh spate of tears.

"The culprit may've been alone, may've snuck upstairs and entered your bedroom without disturbing you. Then taken the babe away and down the stairs and out the front door."

"The door was unbarred when I got up," Miriam agreed. She wiped at her teary face with a linen cloth she retrieved from a nearby table.

Ashurta inspected the room, checking the windows, the shelves, and under the bed. He didn't find any overt evidence of the crime. "Is anything else out of place?"

"I don't think so."

"Then I shall have to interrogate the neighbors next," Ashurta decided. "But first I'm going to check the rest of the house."

"Do so freely," Miriam said.

The slave quarter was neat and orderly if a bit bare. There were no hangings on the walls and the bedding was rough wool and flax cloths. Ashurta checked under the bed and on the shelves where clothes and other items were stacked.

He walked slowly through the rest of the house, and stopped again at the second-story window. It had a latch that could've been easily lifted through the gap in the window and the frame by someone sliding a tool in through the gap and lifting the lever. But the culprit had broken the pane, and he assumed he was working alone, scaling the tree and spiriting through the house like a night spectre. He'd left Miriam alive, but who knew about the babe? Still, he assumed it was a kidnapping, and he'd investigate the entire city if he had to.

The mausoleum was next. He went outside to take the stairs down underground into the carved out mausoleum. It was decorated with statues and the sarcophagi looked like Egyptian styles. The room was cool compared to the rising heat outside.

Nothing seemed to be disturbed, so he returned to the yard and paced the walled confine. There was a disarray in the vines along one section that connected to the main street. "I think here is where the culprit climbed over," he told one of the soldiers who approached. "Look at these footprints in the dust."

"I'll check outside the wall," the soldier said.

The gate looked to be in tact and the rest of the garden wall seemed undisturbed with its flowering vines climbing over it. The rest of the garden had flowering bushes and fruit trees. A garden bench under a trellis for shade was central. A running stream of water with a small paddlewheel provided a cooling effect.

Ashurta traced the path to the tree that connected to the second story window with the broken window. A blue thread was caught on a branch and he climbed up to reach it. "Here," he told the soldier next to him. "Here is evidence. It is fine linen."

He placed the thread in a pouch hanging from his belt.

After one more tour of the garden, he reentered the house and inspected the kitchen. "Are all the knives still here?"

"I … I think so," Miriam hesitated. "In truth, I hadn't checked, but I'll do that now." She searched through the kitchen area under Ashurta's watchful eye. "I don't see my butcher knife."

"What was it like?"

"Bronze handle with carved dragons, and a broad sharp blade for butchering."

"I want you to check the linens next and tell me if they're all there."

A few minutes later, she returned while he inspected the rest of the windows and doors.

"A pillow cover is missing, it was purple. It has our mark."

"Alright," he said. "We're done here. I'm going to leave you these two guards and if you notice anything else, just tell them and they'll get it to me."

The two guards settled onto a low couch in the living room, their weapons clanging against the floor as they sat down.

"They'll be on shifts," Ashurta explained. "They'll contact me if there is more information or if you are in further danger."

"I haven't told anyone else about this. My husband and neighbors don't know yet."

Ashurta scowled. "I will speak to all of them. Everyone you know is now a suspect. I'll send a scribe and you can give him a list of all the people you know and are in contact with, and those that you haven't had contact with for a while. I'll go over the list later."

She rushed up to him and embraced him. "I can't go through this alone."

"When does your husband return?" He patted her back in consolation.

She pulled away from him and looked at all the soldiers in turn. "I don't know. It may be in the next few days. He's a merchant and has his business to conduct," she pouted.

Ashurta put her at arms length but reassured her, "I will be in contact with you soon. I'll report in on what I find out and I want you to try hard to think of anything you haven't told me yet."

She ran a hand over her coif. "I can't think of anything else right now."

Her slave came into the room.

"What is it?" Miriam asked.

"Pardon me, mistress, but will these men be staying for the noonday meal?"

Miriam stood straighter and replied, "There will be two more at the table for the near future. Please plan accordingly."

"Yes, mistress."

"I'm leaving you now," Ashurta said and signaled to the guards.

"I will pray for your success," Miriam said as tears began to flow again. "El be with you."

"I follow Jehovah. He will guide me."

"Whichever god finds my baby I will follow."

He left her with fresh tears in her eyes.

He needed a scribe to send back to Miriam's house, and also one to record his investigation as it started.

He stopped first at the next neighbors. The one on the side of the broken window told him that Miriam had not been alone.

"She is not always alone when her husband is gone," the lady of the house said.

A slave brought beer for them as they sat at the living room table.

It was good beer, and the bread was warm. Ashurta tried the olive oil as a dip and found it only made him hungrier. He refocused on the woman in front of him.

"She has others over when her husband is gone. Last night was no different."

Miriam hadn't mentioned it to him, and he determined to ask her about it next time he saw her, which would likely be soon.

She had been too familiar with him, and so he didn't doubt this woman's story.

"Did you see or recognize who she had over last night?"

"It was a dark haired man with a beard. That's all I could see."

"Could you recognize him again?"

"Not really. I just know that she was with someone."

"The description doesn't help me much. Half the men in Gomorrah fit that description."

"I can watch for him again, and when he is there again, I can go over there and see who he is."

"I don't want you spying on her. I just want to know what you know."

"I don't mind doing it. I'm sure I can find out who he is."

Ashurta considered her and her offer. "Very well. I can be reached at the palace."

"You are staying at the palace?" she marveled.

"I am a cousin to King Birsha, from the city of Ur."

"I have heard of such a place. But didn't it fall?"

Ashurta scowled. Not liking the reminder of his failure to protect the city from the uprising, he snarled, "it did."

"So," she said. "You weren't able to hold that city. What do you think that you can do here?"

Ashurta resented her accusation, but said, "I will do all I can."

He concluded the interrogation on that sour note.

Next he went to the other neighbor's house and sat with the couple and their young family for the noonday meal. Ashurta didn't find out anything from them, and so he headed back to the palace.

# CHAPTER FIVE

When Ashurta entered the great hall, King Birsha bid him to come forward.

Ashurta approached and bowed to him, then straightened. "I've come from the mistress Mariam's house. Her babe appears to have been taken in the night, and I need to send her a scribe to record what occurred. I need one for this investigation. It may take some time."

"You'll have what you need," Birsha said. "This has happened before."

"What was the outcome to the other investigations?"

"They were fruitless," he replied with a saddened expression. Then he pulled himself up straighter on his throne. "You are here now to alleviate this and other situations. This city has grown lawless as you are finding out."

"I will need more soldiers to investigate this and I need to know about the other cases like this."

"The scribe will get you that information from the records. Proceed with your work, but for now I hunger. Let's retire to the dining hall and eat. Come, talk to me while we dine."

Ashurta felt as if he hadn't stopped eating all morning. "I've already eaten."

"Sit with me, then."

Ashurta bowed his head in acquiescence. Then he followed Birsha down the hallway. He intended to excuse himself as soon as he could before the evidence trail grew cold. But for the moment, he'd placate the king.

***

Lilliana pet the temple lion, Shona, on the head as she watched a trail of supplicants enter and leave the temple. Although the lion was tame, the visitors gave her wide berth. It was feeding time for her which especially drew a crowd. Lilliana led Shona into her feeding pen at the rear of the temple, and Tamru the high priest tossed the gazelle meat into her pen. A cheer went up from the gathered crowd.

Making her way back into the temple with her two guards following dutifully, Lilliana tended to the incense in the holy-of-holies before heading to the kitchen to check on the preparations. The crowd of the poor would gather soon and they'd need to be fed.

Leaving the kitchen, she went to the chamber where she intended to work on hymns. She picked up a flute and tested a few notes for the new melody in her mind. Its prose was to the goddess Ishtar, the grand lady. She dipped the pen in the ink well and marked the notes on a piece of papyrus. She hummed it aloud and one of the guard's eyebrows raised at the pleasant tones. A part of her duties was to sing hymns to the people and she had trained her voice. She began to sing the slow melody. It was haunting and intense. She felt tears prick her eyelids as she finished the requiem. The guards were staring at her in awe. She turned to them with a smile.

At the doorway, the temple guard Nodin appeared. "High Priestess, there is a visitor for you." He looked displeased.

Lilliana felt a finger of dread climb her spine. "Who is it?"

"It's Yassib, and he looks angry."

The governor! He couldn't have traced her to his son's death, could he?

"Tell him that I'm unwell," Lilliana lied.

"I'll try." With that, Nodin disappeared down the hall.

A long moment later, she heard the governor and Nodin arguing as they came closer.

The door burst open. The governor stood there fuming.

"Lilliana, there is something for us to discuss urgently," Yassib announced.

"Don't you have more errant slaves to round up today Yassib?" she asked.

He scowled. "I have been told that you are the reason my son is dead," he said.

The guards bristled and reached for their

swords. The wooshing of metal against the scabbards accompanied their pulling the weapons out for display.

"Call down your guard dogs, Lilliana," Yassib soothed. "I know what kind of man my son was. I'm here because I know what happened. His attack got him what he deserved."

Lilliana gasped, and signaled the gaurds to back down. They stepped back a pace.

"I'm sorry about your son," she tried to speak evenly but her voice broke.

"I am not sure I'm sorry. He was becoming a burden and I have seven other sons of which I'm also despairing. I know he tried to harm you."

"I'm sorry," was all that Lilliana could say again. "I would've wished it to come out another way. But what can I do for you to make it up?"

"I want a funeral for him. He'll be buried in the family mausoleum at my house. I want a service though that'll warn off others of his secret order from trying to take over this city as they've been trying to do." He leaned against the doorway.

"Tamru can give the sermon. He is forceful with the inhabitants," Lilliana suggested. She rose from the table and reached for a goblet to fill it with wine for the governor. She handed it to him and he took it gratefully. She poured another one for herself. Noticing that the guards still had their swords drawn, she signaled them with a wave of her hand to put them away.

"That might not be good enough, but I suppose it is all I can get." The governor appeared thoughtful. "I want to write his speech. That should take care of the matter. I know how to control the populace."

"It'll be good to see you using words instead of force like you usually do," Lilliana said.

"My son had gained in the underworld. He'd become a henchman of the upstart prophet trying to come to power."

"I know he was popular. That's why I've been afraid."

"Not of me, I hope," Yassib said, then took a swig from the goblet. He pushed away from the doorframe and began to pace inside the small chamber.

Lilliana felt crowded in her usually sacred space. She placed her goblet down on the table and folded her arms akimbo. "I was afraid of what would happen when you found out about your son," Lilliana said. "Until now."

"It's not me for you to fear, high priestess, but that prophet Godolfin. I don't know where he hides but his following is growing by the day. He predicts things and they come true so that he is getting more and more followers. He has a dark magic that can't be stopped. The longer we wait before doing something about him, the worse off the city will be. Not only this city, but also the sister cities of the vale. I can't think of what to do, though, to stop him. He's like a shadow that is always in back but can never be pinned down. He moves about with the protection of the citizens. I believe he is threatening the king's power also. You must be very careful. If I can find out that you're responsible for my son's death then he can find out, too."

"He is dangerous, too dangerous. He usurps the temple power. I agree. He must be stopped."

"You have spoken true," Yassib said.

"Do you know how to draw him out of hiding?"

"My spies have been useless at finding him. But, it may be that we can use you to do that. If I know of how my son died then he must by now too. Then we can catch him when he comes after you."

"I thought I was in danger from you. Now I realize it's this prophet that I need to worry about. I wasn't certain until now. I have guards with me at all times now, so I don't think that I can plan on meeting him face to face."

"I wouldn't count on that," Yassib said. "But, come. Let's discuss what to do when he does. I'll be there for you."

"I can't thank you enough for understanding," Lilliana stated. "I only wish things were different."

She was unsure what she could do to change the situation, but she felt relieved that she now had the good governor as an ally.

***

Ashurta and his soldiers began scouring the city in organized contingents. Standing together in the courtyard of the palace, they took in Ashurta's orders with typical obedience. Ashurta was accustomed to his men's obedience. They'd followed him in battle in Ur against the uprising and had obeyed him blindly. They were seasoned fighting men, and with the unrest in the city, he knew that they'd be up to the task. They had to go house to house in their searches. He had a thousand soldiers, and there were five thousand houses in the city. It wouldn't take them too long. Ashurta felt confidant that the babe would be found.

"I want every house checked." He ordered the guards into pairs. "Watch eachother's backs."

"There are five thousand houses in this city," one of the imperial guards said. "That is a lot of homes to check. We've had to do searches before."

"There are also visitors to the city. They may be dangerous, too. Check all the inns, also," Ashurta said. He planted his feet firmly and his chest swelled with pride at the good men before him.

He signaled a soldier to his left and he placed down a map of the city on the table in the patio. "We'll divide the city into quadrants. We'll check the wealthy neighborhoods first, that means this inner-city behind the inner-wall where Miriam lives. That fiber we found is high end. The babe has a heart-shaped birthmark on her back. The kidnappers may still contact us for a ransom. But I learned from the king that other babes have been taken and never been returned."

"Call upon Jehovah if you get into trouble," Daniel interjected. "Who knows what you'll encounter in this city."

A rousing cheer went up from the soldiers before they lined up to receive their assigned houses and head out into the city.

After a half day of searching the wealthy quarter, Ashurta gathered with his lieutenants to hear back what they'd uncovered.

The light streamed in through the windows of the pub where Ashurta stopped with his men. They filled the empty table in the noisy room.

"Hail, soldiers," the portly proprietor said to them as he approached the table with a wet cloth and wiped it down. "Do you have your day's barley with you?"

"No, we don't," Daniel answered for them.

"Then you can't be taking up my tables. I have a business to run."

"The palace will pay you," Ashurta interjected, raising his hand to the proprietor. "We work for the king."

The proprietor looked him over, frowning. "Which king? There are several around."

"The king of this city," Ashurta answered sharply.

"That's still not the right answer. There are those in this city that would challenge the throne and consider themselves a king already."

"I only know of one, King Birsha."

The proprietor grinned. "That'll be good enough."

"Before you leave," Ashurta beckoned. "What is this about another claim to the kingship?"

"I hear all kinds of things in here. Especially when the tongues loosen with my supreme beer."

"Treasonous talk, then," Ashurta surmised. He determined to place spies in the beer houses to catch the information. Perhaps he could even find an informant. Meanwhile, he waved the proprietor away. The men needed a break.

A few minutes later, the proprietor began serving them the sacred beer in glazed clay cups. The wooden table groaned as the men leaned their elbows on them and began to eat the bread with olive oil the proprietor placed in front of them.

Ashurta rapped on the tabletop to get everyone's attention. "We have a dire task to finish this day, but I want every man accounted for before we go on with the investigation. Do you each have your counts ready?" He typically required a head count and so he expected his lieutenants to be ready.

He listened as each man relayed the headcounts. Two were missing. "Who has not returned for their noonday meal?" Ashurta asked.

"Brodin and Evber are not back yet," Daniel replied.

"We'll continue on without them." Ashurta rubbed his forehead with a weary hand. "Report in on your findings, starting over here."

One of the men said, "There are reports of stolen goods all over the city. The inhabitants expect the soldiers to stop the burglaries that have been happening. They're increasing, we're told."

"What else?" Ashurta asked.

Halfway through the reporting, it was Daniel's turn. He said, "There are disturbing rumors that have been told this day. There is a false prophet riling the city up. Lord Godolfin, they call him. He is prophesying that he will inherit the throne. It had the wealthy quadrant worked up this morning as their servants and slaves have been talking about this new prophet they want to be king."

"The Lady Gracilga talked of this, and now you hear more. What else do we know about this prophet?" Ashurta worried over the city being divided. It reminded him of Ur. He'd failed to stop the uprising there and he wondered if he could stop one here in Gomorrah. It was an unknown city to him, and yet he'd understood Ur well. But Gomorrah evidently had other undercurrents running through it with the castes of people. He clenched his fists and said, "it may be an entirely different problem, but one we'll have to deal with in the future if he's threatening to take King Birsha's throne from him." But could he protect his cousin the king? Let alone the city itself.

"I'll ask around more tomorrow about these prophecies, then," Daniel offered, dipping bread into the olive oil and taking a bite, looking nonplussed.

"Better to start today," Ashurta replied.

"Today we're busy with the search for the baby. Maybe the men should focus on one thing at a time," Daniel said, cocking an eyebrow.

Scowling at Daniel that he'd question his orders, Ashurta moved on. "All of you do so while you're out among the populace this afternoon. It'll save time having to reinvestigate again right away. Now, let's get back to it."

The soldiers around the table thumped their fists to their chests in homage, and rose to leave.

Ashurta arranged for payment with the proprietor, then followed the lieutenants out as they sent the troops on the search again.

He searched alongside a soldier who'd been very young when he joined up. Ashurta prided himself on knowing each of his thousand personally to some degree. He'd wanted that as a young soldier himself coming up through the ranks in Abraham's army. Turning to the youth, he asked, "Adelabad, have you decided what you think of this city? Compared to what you remember about Ur. I know you were very young there."

"I've thought that perhaps I'm not valued in this city, Lord Ashurta." He rubbed his neck absently as they marched along the road towards the east side of the city.

"It is a curious populace. I warn you to remain alert to its nuances. It could turn on any of you at any moment. Here is where we left off on this morning's searches," Ashurta said as they came to a doorway painted red.

"I remember it," Adelabad said. "Do you think this is dye, or blood stain?"

"It is rather curious. We'll find out now."

Pounding at the door, Ashurta barked, "Open this door now for an inspection by the king's sovereigns."

A moment later the door was wrenched open. A curious red-bearded man stood in the way, and Ashurta and his young soldier pushed past.

"Stand back for the inspection," Ashurta said.

The man eyed their uniforms and weapons, then asked, "Why do you bother me? I've done nothing."

"What is on your doorway," Adelabad pursued. "Is that dye or blood?"

The red-bearded chin dropped. "It is a custom here to use both. It cements the gods' support. Where are you from that you don't know this?"

"Where we're from is irrelevant," Ashurta interjected. "Do you know where any babies are at? We're searching for one this morning."

Adelabad began searching the main room of the small house, looking under the piles of cloth and cushions around the main fire pit with facetious gestures.

"I don't have any children, and I don't care where any are," the red-bearded man stated. "I'm out of work right now, and unless you have some to give me, you are just harbingers of bad fortune."

"Where is your family and slaves?" Ashurta asked.

Adelabad checked the kitchen area next, looking into all the shelves, and tossing earthenware out of the way. Several crashed to the wooden floor.

"Watch what you're doing in there," the man shouted. "That isn't necessary."

"You must hear rumors in this city, as you're going about searching for work," Ashurta said. He stepped closer to the man, and wrinkled his nose at the smell. Peering into his narrowed eyes, he added, "if you tell me what you've heard it'll go easier on you."

Adelabad made his way to the ladder leading to the upstairs bedroom. He put a foot on the lowest rung and tested it as if he was unsure it would hold his weight.

"I only know rumors, as you say," the man said.

Climbing to the top, Adelabad called down, "It's a mess up here. Give me a minute or two."

"Well?" Ashurta prodded.

"It is only rumor about the stolen infants, but it is said that they are new moon sacrifices." The man had the good grace to shudder as his eyes widened with hysteria.

"What?" Ashurta was aghast. He'd realized there must be foul play with so many infants gone, but for them to be sacrificed spoke of a vile city, indeed. "Where do these sacrifices take place?"

"I don't know. I only do animal sacrifices," he stepped back a pace, running up against the plaster wall with scenes of dancers on it.

"Why do you sacrifice outside the temple?" Ashurta asked, fondling the pommel of his sword.

The man glanced sideways. "It is the way of my sect. We follow the moon god but he's been forgotten by the high priest and high priestess. We follow a different way." Shuddering again, he added, "it's no crime."

"We'll see about that. I'll check on the laws regarding sacrificing and I'll be back if I find out you are breaking the law." Ashurta was seeing red and reflexively grasped the hilt of his sword.

Just then, Adelabad returned. "There's no sign of an infant in this house, Lord Ashurta."

"See that you report to me at the palace if you hear more of those rumors," Ashurta stressed as they left for the next house.

He'd just learned of a horror going on, and he was now bound to stop the human sacrifices. Turning his thoughts to Jehovah, he prayed inwardly that the rumors might not be true. But even as he thought it, he felt the sacrifices must be real.

\*\*\*

The soldiers filed back to the palace at dusk and Ashurta awaited reports. Some of the soldiers still hadn't reported in yet by the time he had to go to dinner with the king.

The next morning, Ashurta gathered his soldiers again.

"Where are Brodin and Evber?" someone asked.

"Didn't they check in at the barracks?" Ashurta asked.

"They didn't come back last night," another soldier said.

"Then look for them today while you quiz the merchants."

"Aye, general," the chorus went up.

Only a hundred of his soldiers were paired up the same as the day before to do the remainder of the searches. "Men, take the remaining houses in the worst quadrant of the city next. Check them all. Check the slave quarters in the houses, first. I suspect these kidnappings are about that. Any questions?"

One soldier spoke up, "What about the slave quarters in the wealthy homes?"

"I'll be doing the rest of the upper class searches personally," Ashurta said. "I'll take Hoeneb with me."

His red-headed seargent at arms stepped forward. "I'm prepared."

"This is going to be dangerous," Ashurta said. "Keep armed at all times, and don't be afraid to use force where necessary."

"The populace erupts into disorder quickly," Hoeneb added.

"True," Ashurta agreed. "Keep reporting in every four hours until the search is done. And don't come back without our missing soldiers."

"What if we don't find anything?" one of the soldiers asked.

"We'll find something," Ashurta reassured. "Keep the faith in Jehovah."

With the instructions done, Ashurta sent the men forth. He turned to Hoeneb. "Tell my brother that we are leaving and he is to stay with King Birsha."

"Aye," Hoeneb said. Turning to do Ashurta's bidding, he left Ashurta alone.

Ashurta poured himself a cup of tea from the carafe on the nearby table. It was turning out to be a hard search, but he was determined. This city was out of control and he'd start here and now to change that. After all, Jehovah was on his side.

***

Lilliana reached for her sleeveless robe and donned it, then placed the lapis lazuli jewelry on her neck. Next, she added the pentagram talisman of her royal rank, and an Egyptian bracelet with a carnelian scarab above her elbow. She examined her reflection, then turned to leave her bed chamber.

It was an ordinary day in the temple and many mundane tasks needed to be seen to. She stepped slowly down the stairs, careful not to trip on her long robe and her guards trailed her a few paces behind. At the bottom, she looked to the side of the main hall at the scribe school in progress. Shona the lioness was lounging nearby, awaiting her morning feeding time. The crowds that liked to watch her would gather soon.

As she walked past the scribe school to go to the kitchen, she spotted a youth standing to the side, watching. She recognized him from the kitchen deliveries, and she caught his eye.

Signaling him over, she whispered, "What do you need, Keret?"

The lanky youth scratched his thin beard. "Well, I want to join the scribe school." He shook back his long hair.

"I don't know when the next session will start, and you need a sponsor. It is an elite profession, after all." She didn't want to discourage him, just remind him of how it was.

She beckoned him to follow her. Winding their way to the kitchen, she gathered up a breakfast for herself and Keret and walked outside to a table just beyond the kitchen door. It looked out onto the patio garden of flowering plants. The fruit trees were also laden, and the birds were pecking at the bounty. Butterflies abounded, and dragonflies drawn to the interspersed fountains.

"Sit with me, Keret," she said.

There were silk cusions on the stonework benches around the table. Something from the tithes of the city.

"Oh, great High Priestess," Keret said. "Can you sponsor me for the scribe school?"

Lilliana stopped midway to taking a bite of barley bread. "I haven't been anyone's sponsor for it before. I'm not certain I could."

"Yes, you could," he cajoled, pushing at his plate of food. "It has to work. You're prestigious enough for them to take you seriously."

"I suppose I can ask them," she offered. "Find out what their requirements are these days."

"I'm prepared to work very hard at it. Why, if I have to tote one more load of barley to the temple I think I'll die."

She laughed at him, then felt badly for it and said, "I think you won't die. We all have our work in the city."

"That's not true. You've seen the poor. They come here because they have nothing else and no work. The elites get fat off of them when they do work. It isn't fair."

"Then why are you so anxious to join the elites, if you are so bitter about them."

"I can change them, make them see the errors of their ways. While I work as a scribe, of course, so they'll take me seriously."

"You have such an interest in the politics of the city, perhaps there are other ways you can influence for the better."

"I'm only a youth. What else can I do? The city needs to change. Anyone can see that."

"I will see what I can do. Now, eat, so that you have strength for your deliveries today. Good things will come to you in time."

They ate in silence then until she left him for the rest of her day.

\*\*\*

The exorcism later in the morning required a few things, and Lilliana gathered them while she hummed to herself. The victim was in the poorest section of the city and so there wasn't likely to be compensation for the service she was about to perform. But the temple was the last bastion of charity in the city, and she signaled her two guards and headed out onto the street. Gracilga met her at the entrance to accompany her on the event. Five hundred paces after leaving the temple, they came to the right house. The two guards were within arm's reach the whole time.

It was shrouded in black to keep out the bright sunlight. As Lilliana entered the gloom, one of the soldiers followed her inside. He took up position by the wooden door, and looked about the one-story house with disdain.

Lilliana and Gracilga greeted the two women in the main room that was combined with the dining area. The kitchen and food storage area were on the other side of a partition dividing the rooms. The aroma of the morning's barley porridge still hung in the air.

The woman afflicted was on the low couch clasping her arms about herself and shaking. Her stringy blonde hair clung to the sides of her face.

The other woman was sitting to her side an arm's length away, perched on the edge of the couch. "Oh, great High Priestess, you've come at last," she said with a cry. "My sister is in agony. You must help her."

"I'll need some herbs boiled. Can you do that now?" Lilliana asked, digging into her satchel for the ingredients. "Set these to boil then I'll tell you what to do."

"Yes, High Priestess."

Lilliana approached the shaking woman. "Selene, what are you feeling now?"

The woman simply shook her head.

"I need to know what is going on," Lilliana coaxed.

Her sister reentered the room, and said, "She is possessed, can't you tell?"

"Gracilga, can you help her with the herbs?"

"I will," Gracilga said. She reached for the sister and pushed her back into the kitchen area. "That is the best thing you can do," she told her.

"Selene, speak to me about what is happening to you," Lilliana inched closer to the woman.

Trembling, she answered, "I'm cursed. The money has been getting stolen, and disappears when I'm looking for it. The meat has been growing worms when I've just bought it fresh that morning. Blood has been appearing on my clothes when I'm not cut. I can't sleep because I hear terrible sounds in the night that no one else hears. I'm possessed by something wicked that won't let go."

"I'll help you now, don't worry any longer Selene."

Gracilga and the sister returned with the steaming pot.

"Place it on the side table next to Selene," Lilliana said.

Gracilga returned to her side. "What can I do now?"

"You've done enough by alerting me to this woman's travail." She addressed Selene, "Will you give up this evil spirit now and send it into the wilderness?"

"Yes, High Priestess."

Lilliana reached into her satchel for the ceremonial bread and tore it into chunks. "Then spit onto these pieces and deliver them to the desert for the scavengers today."

"But, High Priestess," the sister said. "Selene isn't fit to travel."

"You can deliver it for her, if you want."

"Give me the bread," Selene said.

Lilliana handed her two pieces.

Selene spit onto both and then handed them to her sister who wrapped them into a linen cloth.

"I'll go now to the desert," the sister said.

"Will this work, High Priestess?" Selene asked quietly, a tear rolling down her cheek.

"It always does. When the scavengers eat the bread, the evil spirit will go into their bodies and leave you alone. You won't be bothered anymore."

Gracilga moved to the door. "I'll walk back

to the temple with you."

Lilliana nodded to all the women and they departed.

They made their way slowly through the crowds on the streets near the center of the city, before the inner-wall. The soldiers flanked Lilliana and Gracilga closely, taking their arms at one point to guide them through the crush of people. And for good reason.

A melee started up in front of merchants at the marketplace as they reached it. Merchants rushed to pull their wares inside their houses lining the street and to cover their carts of wares. Fighting erupted and the soldiers pulled the ladies off down a side alley where many were rushing to flee the melee.

Lilliana had wanted to check on the pregnant cloth merchant, but couldn't get close to her now with the violent situation, so she jogged along beside the soldiers with her friend.

They wound around the alleys until they came to the temple rising up like a hillock. It's blooming gardens were casting their floral scent on the hot wind, and Lilliana appreciated the sedate beauty of the terraces layered with foliage. She held her hand to her brow to shield herself from the sun that was now high overhead. Moisture beaded along her forehead and down her back from running in the heat. The soldiers slowed to a walk and they all entered the temple.

The cool and colorful inside buoyed Lilliana up after the fright of the marketplace, a happenstance that was occurring with increased frequency. The violence in the city was erupting in more times and places. Lilliana felt despair at it well up inside her but she spontaneously hugged Gracilga warmly as if to ward off the currents of the city. Gracilga babbled on about things and Lilliana felt that all could be right in the world again, if only the gods would hear her pleas to return peace to the city. Maybe she should question Ashurta more about his god. It couldn't hurt.

# CHAPTER SIX

Now that they were back, Lilliana headed toward the scribe class and approached the teacher. He looked up from surveying the students' work, raising an eyebrow.

"Ibu-gal," Lilliana inquired. "May I have a word with you?"

"This is the middle of class, High Priestess. It'll have to wait."

"This is about class. You've just started this new session. Will you take on a new student? He is very eager."

"Not the barley boy again, I hope."

"It is."

"Then I shall have to decline. Again."

"How disappointing. Surely you can reconsider?" Lilliana cajoled. Behind her, Gracilga emitted a disappointed sound, but remained back.

"I've already started this class session and don't want to spend time catching up with a late student. Besides, I think that young man needs to set his sights elsewhere. There's a reason the gods placed him as a delivery boy and not a scribe by birth."

"I don't see why he couldn't ascend from his echelon, in time. He has a positive attitude."

"Yes, yes, but that doesn't make it the right thing to do."

"Won't you reconsider?" she asked.

"Not today. Not tomorrow. If things change, approach me again. I only want high caliber students here. Now good day to you."

Disgruntled, Lilliana looked at Gracilga who'd been hovering and nodded to her to follow her. They made their way to the kitchen for the noonday meal. Gracilga could help her with preparing the food to be distributed to the poor later in the day.

They worked side by side, alongside the other kitchen workers preparing food from the day's offerings and talked of better times.

*** 

Ashurta and Daniel wended their way through the city's labyrinthine streets, searching houses randomly as they went, repeating after yesterday hoping to catch the culprits unawares. The buildings were very close together, overshadowing the street. The residents in this quarter were surly and uncooperative with them. Ashurta had to draw his sword more than once. As they were exiting a house with crumbling plaster over the exposed stonework, the door slammed behind them.

"There's a crowd over there, overflowing into that alley," Daniel pointed out. He'd talked his way into accompanying Ashurta instead of remaining with King Birsha.

"Likely something they wouldn't want us to see them up to," Ashurta said.

They strode towards the crowd, and at the edge of it, they pushed through to round a corner. The boisterous group was looking upward and several were heckling.

Ashurta felt shock wash over him as he followed their gazes and his landed on a cage suspended overhead above the ground. It was about four cubits by four cubits, and suspended from a tall oak tree. Inside he could make out two men, stripped naked.

"Ashurta," one of the imprisoned men called out. "It's me, Brodin."

Daniel pointed unnecessarily to the cage. "Look, Ashurta, it's our missing soldiers."

"By all that is holy, let's get them down."

Pushing through the crowd further, they spotted the tied rope that was holding the cage up, tied to a nearby smaller olive tree. Ashurta reached for his sword and sliced through the rope in a fell swoop.

The cage came crashing down on the crowd which broke the fall. The people backed up and the ones trapped underneath groaned in agony.

"Out of the way," Daniel shouted. He pushed his way to the cage and sliced open the rope holding the door closed.

"What is the meaning of this?" One of the onlookers yelled, echoed by several more voices.

"What are you doing?"

"They're visitors to the city."

"They deserve it."

"They were snooping around our houses."

Several of the men calling out were armed, and surged forward to challenge Ashurta and Daniel who came to blows with one of them. He swung his sword in an arc and sliced off the forearm of one of the threatening men. The man howled in pain and outrage, falling to the ground.

"Who's next?" Ashurta barked, parrying his sword around him while the two Hebrews in the cage crawled out.

Brodin said, "General, we were waylaid yesterday and were left in the cage to die up there."

"Yes, General," Evber said. "They apparently treat their visitors to the city to the cages."

"Despicable," Ashurta said. Pushing through the crowd again, he led the two naked battered soldiers through while Daniel held up the rear.

The crowd suddenly surged forward and attempted to outnumber the Hebrews.

Ashurta parried against a few weapons close to him, and meted out deadly blows. The bodies falling tripped up the rest of the crowd from getting closer to him.

The naked soldiers were wrestling with men and doing hand to hand combat they'd been trained for in Ur for close city fighting.

Daniel was killing as many as he could with vigor.

Just then, the sound of a horn blasted over the air. The governor sat on horseback and his personal army stood at one edge of the crowd. "Disperse now, or suffer the consequences," Yassib ordered.

The crowd still struggled to reach the Hebrews so the governor ordered his men forward.

The clash of metal on metal rang out like macabre tones.

The crowd started falling back, and the edges of it started running away. The governor's army made short work of it, and in a few minutes Ashurta hacked the last attacker to death.

"Governor Yassib," Ashurta smoothed back his long hair out of his eyes, flicking sweat to the side. "We're indebted to you and your army."

The governor dismounted and grasped arms with Ashurta. "It is a debt I will hold you too. One can't have too many allies in this forsaken city. I know of what I speak."

"My men and I will now count you as friend. In fact, you can rely upon my people from now on. Word of your deed here today will travel far and wide," Ashurta said.

"Fair of you," Yassib said. "Now you and your injured men better get back to the palace before the crowd reforms up or worse tries to ambush you at another quarter."

"Say you will join us there with your army later for a thanksgiving meal."

"We will be honored. Let King Birsha know

that we'll be there for dinner."

"Come along, men," Ashurta said. He felt terrible for his battered soldiers, but they were professionals and had been trained for hardships. He couldn't do anything about the fact that he wanted to protect his men from harm. From time to time, some would inevitably fall, but not for a very long time if he had anything to do with it.

\*\*\*

Lilliana excused herself from the food preparation work to go light incense in the holy of holies. The temple was bustling, and she couldn't shake the sense that she was being watched. She shook it off. Of course she was getting attention from the bevy of onlookers, including those in the patio. Some were still lined up for potential work for the day. The scribe class was just breaking up for the day. Supplicants were greeting the high priest out front. The temple guards were strolling amid the crowd.

Her own guards were only a pace behind. Still, the finger of dread made it's way up her spine. She entered past the curtain of the holy of holies, hurried through the incense lighting, then bumped one of her guards unintentionally as she exited.

"Excuse me," she said.

He frowned, but nodded.

"Have you noticed anyone getting too close to the holy of holies?" she asked, rubbing her hands together. With the death of the governor's son still weighing on her, she felt a flicker of consternation that she didn't know if retaliation would be coming. Again. After losing her first guard to an attack, she worried over the others that took their posts.

"I noted no one, High Priestess," the Hebrew soldier replied.

"I suppose I'm just nervous."

"That's what I'm here for." His smile was genuine.

"Follow me while I take a walk around the temple and check on things."

Later, she met up with Gracilga again in front of the kitchen.

"I want to find out about Neanna's upcoming birth," she told Gracilga. "By my calcuations, she should be delivering soon. I had hoped to stop by to see her on the way back here, but the uprising was in the way."

"We could try going by later on to see if anything has happened," Gracilga suggested.

"No, there is more to do to distribute the food, and I can use your help here for it. I'll send one of the guards to check on her now. After. that riot, I want to find out the news."

"Alright, if you're sure. We could always go and return quickly."

"No, if she's delivered, we can take food to her later on. Then we can visit with her and I can bless the baby."

"If you think so."

Lilliana smiled at her friend and looked around for the nearest temple guard. Meanwhile, her own bodyguards were still shadowing her. She spotted Nodin and called him over from his patrol about the public patio. She walked toward him and asked him to go to the courtyard with her. With Gracilga following, they stopped next to the bronze sea, the font of water sitting atop twelve life-sized bronze bulls. It was for sacred cleansing of the temple and was revered by the people surrounding it, dipping their hands into it and splashing their faces with the holy water. She asked Nodin, "Can you do a special errand?"

"What is it you need, High Priestess?" He'd been distant since the happenings with the death of the governor's son, and he peered at her intently.

"Can you go to the marketplace to see Neanna the cloth merchant and find out if she has delivered her baby yet?" Lilliana reached into her pouch on her belt and drew out a chunk of lapis. She handed it to Nodin. "Please?"

"I have to finish this patrol, but then I can go do it." He clutched the valuable stone.

"Thank you, Nodin."

"Thank you, High Priestess," he said cheerfully.

"Come, Gracilga, let's begin serving the food to the poor. It's the only meal some of them get for the day."

"Good works will surely be blessed by the gods," Gracilga said.

"It is true, and the people of the city would do well to remember that." She strode through the crowd in the courtyard, noting the guards closing in to push people aside.

"I could never get used to bodyguards," Gracilga quipped.

"I don't know how long I'll need them."

"What have you heard about the danger?"

"It's still imminent, but I can't let it slow me down. I have many duties, and the people overall still respect me. I suppose the danger will pass."

"I wouldn't be so sure about that," Gracilga said doubtfully. "What with that prophet Godolfin leading the uprisings. Rumor is that he's up to many foul deeds. You won't be safe for a long time to come."

"I sincerely hope that you're wrong. Come. Let us attend to the poor."

\*\*\*

After a meeting updating him on the progress within the city, Godolfin called in three of his followers. The cave was cooler than anywhere else in the city and he strode to the entrance to look out on Gomorrah. "Come with me," he said.

"I'm in a hurry, my lord," the ape of a man said.

"You, men," he said. "Follow that high priestess and capture her. The last two failed, but you must succeed.

The taller ape shook his head. "But she has more guards now."

"I will bless you that you will win out over them." Godolfin reached into his pouch strapped to his waist and withdrew three pearls. "These will be your talismans. You may keep them."

"Daytime she has allies. We can't get near her," the shortest man said even as he took the pearl and polished it on his sleeve.

"I have been scrying and she will be out this night." Godolfin drew in a sharp breath. "Now I will hear no more of this. Be gone. And don't fail me or you will pay with your lives."

"Yes, my lord," the men mumbled together.

They hurried away from their harsh lord.

Godolfin frowned, wishing that the scrying had shown him the outcome tonight. The powers of the royal bloodlines had been fading with each generation, and he thanked the gods that his blood still served him in this well. He would soon conquer, with the gods' help.

\*\*\*

When Nodin returned later in the afternoon, he carried news of Neanna's recent birth.

Lilliana prepared a basket of food and told her guards they'd be travelling through the city after dark to visit Neanna. Gracilga decided to come along, and after the poor were fed their evening meal, the ladies headed back out into the city.

They found the cart in front of Neanna's house empty and not open for business, of course. They passed behind it and knocked on the embellished wooden door. Anisha the midwife opened the door.

"High Priestess and Lady Gracilga, this is not a good time."

"Neanna," Lilliana called through the open door. "Are you here?"

"High Priestess," Neanna called back. "Do

come in. I was just having some help from Anisha, but we can continue later."

"Very well," Anisha said. "She seems to be feeling up to it."

Lilliana and Gracilga entered. The three-story house had an open loft with a stair along one wall. The rest of the downstairs was open and arranged around a low round table and short golden chairs. The jewel-toned cushions on the chairs and on the black couch where Neanna was lying brightened up the dark room. Various candles and tall bronze candelabra were lit, casting the space in dancing shadows.

The house didn't smell of cooking, Lilliana noted. She hefted the full basket onto the table, and turned back to the doorway to tell the guards that she'd be a little while. Anisha closed the door behind them.

"Now, what is this about?" Anisha asked.

"We are just here for a visit, and to deliver some food. Where is this new baby?"

"He is in the corner in the cradle," Anisha answered.

Lilliana and Gracilga approached the sleeping infant. He lay amid swaddling cloths and some flower petals.

"He is a comely babe," Lilliana approved. "He favors your husband, Neanna."

At the mention of her husband, Neanna teared up, and sniffed. "He won't be home for awhile. His new master is working him very hard. I wish I could do something for him."

"He can earn his freedom sooner if he works

more now," Gracilga offered with a tentative smile.

"That's not helpful right now when I need him to help me with the cart and the new baby."

"It is your first child," Anisha said. "You'll learn to make do soon. We were just talking about such things."

"Neanna," Lilliana said. "I'd like to bless the baby now."

"He should be blessed according to our custom," Neanna said.

"I'll do that now while Gracilga prepares you a plate of food from the basket. You must be hungry."

"Thank you, High Priestess. I haven't had the energy to do any cooking, and I'll feel better knowing my son has received his birth blessing."

Lilliana nodded. She removed a vial of oil from her satchel and proceeded to dot her fingertip with the oil. Then she sang the prayer of birth and rubbed the oil on the infant's forehead. He set up squalling and she lifted him and rocked him tenderly, then handed him to his mother.

"I thank you," Neanna said again. "If only my husband could've been here for it. I'd do anything to free him from the slavery. I don't think he'll ever recover from it."

"There's nothing you can do to change it. It is the way of it," Gracilga said as she arranged the food on the table.

"But I'd do anything. Even give up my son if I could have my husband back whole again."

"Be patient, and his time will be up by and by," Lilliana said.

"I wish the king would abolish slavery," Neanna said.

"It is part of our economy right now," Lilliana said. "Perhaps another way can be found. I'd prefer for it to end, too."

"I know that the king is your brother, but I've heard of another man who would be king. They say he is of royal blood, and a prophet. He says he'd free the slaves."

"It is just talk right now, but he is a dangerous man. Godolfin is his name and I know of him because he is stirring up the city. You should be cautious about following such a one."

"I just want my husband freed," Neanna cried.

Lilliana frowned. She stepped over to the table and picked up the basket. "Now we must go. I have much still to do at the temple tonight. Just be careful who you follow."

They parted with the guards pacing them across the marketplace. As they came to an alleyway that was a shortcut to the temple, three shadows moved out of the darkness.

One of the soldiers commanded, "Stand to the side."

The three shadows moved into position in front of them and blocked their path.

Lilliana heard the soldier's swords drawn and saw the outline of the strangers' scimitars flash under the starlight.

"Give us the priestess and you'll live," the bigger man ordered. He took a step forward to reach for her.

Lilliana jumped back with unladylike oath, the basket banging against her hip. "You can't take me."

She pulled out her dagger from its scabbard on her belt, and made a defensive stance.

"The high priestess stays with us," one of her guards said.

"Then fight we will," the bigger man threatened.

The three men moved in and two of them clashed with the guards in sword fighting.

Clanging metal resounded, and onlookers from the end of the alleyway began shouting and moving in to watch the action.

Lilliana avoided the third man as he rushed her and hopped to the side. Instead, he turned about and grabbed Gracilga who screamed and pummeled him.

"No!" Lilliana cried.

The men were fighting and the third man spat out, "Give yourself up, High Priestess or your friend will die!"

Lilliana dropped the basket and made to grab Gracilga and pull her back, but the abductor swung her away.

Lilliana clutched her dagger tightly, wondering what to do, fear causing her to break out in a sweat. She swiped away a drop, and prayed quickly to El to protect her friend.

The guard closest to her struck a deadly blow to his opponent and the scimitar clattered to the ground. He lunged to help his compatriot and he stabbed the opponent with the tip of his sword.

The man went down with a cry of agony, clasping his side and rolling on the ground.

The man clutching Gracilga shouted an inaudible cry and pulled his scimitar across Gracilga's neck. She slumped to the ground with eyes wide open in disbelief. Unspoken words gurgled out of her mouth.

Lilliana screamed in outrage as the assailant took off running. She rushed to Gracilga's side and cradled her lifeless body, tears streaming down her cheeks and falling onto Gracilga's fine silk robe.

One of the guards set to chasing the murderer on fleet feet. He caught him in a few paces and spun the man around. They parried and fought on for some minutes until the guard sliced his sword hand and the scimitar fell to the ground.

"On the ground," the guard ordered.

"Don't hurt me," the man begged.

"You're coming with us."

The second guard reached out to Lilliana and touched her shoulder. "High Priestess, we'll go the castle now."

Placing her friend's body down delicately, she stood. She looked to the crowd that had gathered. She pointed at a big man in the front. "You, there. Carry this woman to the palace with us."

"Alright," he said and approached Gracilga. He hefted her over his shoulder and the two guards and their prisoner turned back to the marketplace's main thoroughfare to make their way to the palace.

When they got there, the guards called out to the palace guards and explained their situation.

The palace guards rushed to the prisoner and took him off to the dungeon.

Another set of palace guards replaced them. "King Birsha is out in the city right now," one of them said.

"Where is Lord Ashurta?" Lilliana asked. Surely he'd know what to do.

"He is in his room," the palace guard answered.

"Rouse him," she said. "This requires his attention."

"Yes, High Priestess," one of the guards said.

When the guard had left, Lilliana turned to the other men. "Did either of you get hurt?"

Both shook their heads and she spoke to the man carrying Gracilga, "Place her body down over on that bench. I want the general to look at her so he can see what that attacker did."

Rushing footsteps behind her caught her attention.

"Lady Lilliana," Ashurta exclaimed. "What has happened?" He threw his arms open wide as he neared and she flew into them.

"It's Gracilga, they murdered her," she said in a voice muffled from his robe. Tears flowed afresh and she peered up at him. "You must avenge her."

Placing her at arms length, Ashurta scowled at the two Hebrew guards. "What happened?"

"We were attacked in an alley. Ambushed. Two of the attackers are dead, and the third one is alive. He's in the dungeon now. He's the one who killed the Lady Gracilga."

Ashurta strode over to the bench where Gracilga lay. He pushed back her hair clinging to her bloodied neck and let out an expletive. "Guard," he turned to the temple guard hovering. "Get me a scribe and send a runner to intercept the king at his party. He needs to know of this right away."

"Aye, general."

Returning to Lilliana's side, Ashurta swept her back into his arms and she clung to him. She only wished he could make things right again.

# CHAPTER SEVEN

The next morning, Ashurta set out again to investigate the missing infant. He took Daniel with him, but arranged with his soldiers to report back in at the noonday meal. He didn't want a repeat of finding the soldiers caged again. He'd sent out soldiers on a variety of tasks for the day handling uprisings and other crimes.

Ashurta had some places to check again, based upon the reports he'd gotten back that the people hadn't been readily forthcoming.

Stopping in at one of the houses in the middle-class section of the city just outside the inner-city wall, Ashurta challenged the occupants. They refused him entry.

While Ashurta began to negotiate with the house occupants, Daniel pushed past the doorway, leading the way in.

Ashurta saw the flash of lamp light on a knife and withdrew his sword.

"Put the knife away," he ordered the occupant, a burly man with a short dark beard.

Daniel slowly withdrew his own sword and stepped forward into the main room of the three-story house. "We're going to inspect your house, and you'll cooperate or pay the consequences."

Ashurta glanced at him, then as the offending knife was put away, he said, "I want to know if you know anything about kidnapped babies from the upper class."

"There are no babies here," the surly head of the house said.

"None at all," the woman garbed in typical purple replied. She stepped back further into the room, angling towards the kitchen.

The layout of the house was of one open room, and to the left was a kitchen divided from the storage room by a screen and pillars. In the center of the floor was a fire pit where a spit was roasting a chicken. The smoke curled upward in a ribbon to the opening in the ceiling.

Ashurta paced the room as he looked it over, and then tested the ladder up to the bedroom above the kitchen area. "I'll inspect the upstairs first, Daniel."

"I'll guard them here." Daniel stepped in front of the door, the only exit from the room. His sword arm stayed ready.

Ashurta nodded, and sheathed his sword to climb the ladder. The bedroom was neat if colorful. It held baskets lining the walls with folded clothes and blankets. He inspected each one, and came to the last basket. In it, he found a purple blanket of linen and wool with the mark of the household he was there in behalf of. It was a crescent moon shape with a gold stripe.

Rage flooded through him like a great wave crashing on the sandy shore. It was obvious this household was hiding something of the baby here. He sucked in a deep breath and cocked his ear to hear what was going on downstairs. He heard Daniel barking orders to the two people to lift cushions on the low couches.

He tucked the blanket under his arm, and descended the ladder. The scowl on his face forewarned Daniel who held the man at sword-tip now.

"I've found the missing blanket," Ashurta growled. "Explain how you got it."

"It was given to us," the woman shouted.

"It was a gift from a friend," the man added.

"It was stolen with an infant, and I'm arresting you –"

Just then, the woman scooted a couple of paces into the kitchen and Ashurta heard the floorboard creek.

"Remove yourself from the kitchen," he barked at her.

"Leave my wife alone," the man said without conviction.

"Do as I say, now," Ashurta ordered.

Hesitating, she stepped over to her husband's side. Her face puckered like she was about to weep.

Daniel stood ground. "Go ahead, I've got them."

Ashurta nodded. He tread into the kitchen where he heard the planks creek, so he thudded his boot heel onto them. He spaced out four boards in each direction. He bent down to fit his pommel into the grooves. The first board came up without a hitch. He tossed it aside.

Glaring into the dark hole, he saw a pythos jar under the floorboards he'd marked. Prying up the others, he lugged the pythos jar with the cork lid onto the floor. "What have we here?"

"It is stored wine, for special occasions. Nothing for you to worry about," the woman lied.

"I don't hear wine inside," he said as he shook it.

Popping off the wide cork, he bent to the opening, and caught bile rising in his throat.

Inside was a dead infant. Buried under the floorboards for only a short time. He held the jar upside down and out slid the tiny carcass. It hit the floor with a thud. Ashurta used the cloth to lift the baby up. "This is what we're searching for." He turned the baby over onto its back.

The man choked out, "We don't know anything about it."

Daniel let out an expletive and pricked the neck of the man with a tiny thrust. "Save your lies, man."

Ashurta inspected the dead baby and found the heart-shaped birthmark on its back where he expected. "What have you done to her?"

The woman began wailing, and the man shouted, "It wasn't us. Have mercy." He held his hand to the tiny prick on his neckline. His beard wiggled as his chin quivered.

"Why should I spare you when I've caught you with the body. This baby looks like it was impaled. That's a sacrificial torture, and a killing method. I've only heard of such things."

Daniel roared, "If you didn't do this, who did?"

"Godolfin the new prophet told us we had to sacrifice."

"There are animals that are traditionally sacrificed by the Kenaani, not infants." Ashurta's rage enflamed. "Human sacrifice was stopped long ago."

"Then you don't understand this city. Or the other cities," the man pleaded.

"I'm arresting you for this murder unless you can produce this prophet."

"I don't know where he lives," the man begged. "Spare my wife, she isn't responsible."

"She's as responsible as you," Ashurta said. "She was hiding it here."

Daniel pulled lengths of chord from his pack and tied the hands of the prisoners.

Ashurta unfolded the blanket he'd retrieved and wrapped the dead baby up.

"How many more infants have been sacrificed?" He didn't expect an answer and got none.

He and Daniel herded the couple off to the palace dungeon. The neighbors came out to watch them pass.

"Come back with some help afterward, Daniel," Ashurta said. "Interview those neighbors and find out what they know about these sacrifices."

"Aye, Ashurta. They'd better be free with their information or it won't go well for them."

Ashurta felt his heart sink. The work in the city was worse than he'd anticipated, and not likely to get better anytime soon. He straightened his shoulders as they headed back to the palace. "Do what you must, Daniel."

***

Godolfin paced the confines of the luxurious room in his present house, the second such house this month alone, while awaiting his envoy. His wait was interrupted by a distraught looking messenger. "Speak up. What is it?" Godolfin asked, upset by the messenger's appearance.

The disheveled messenger prostrated himself, then looked up at Godolfin. "The Hebrews, my lord."

"Well?" Godolfin put his hands behind his back and stood with his feet apart as though he was inspecting a troop. "What have they done now?"

"They found the sacrifices." The messenger rose to his knees. "In the houses."

"What?" Godolfin threw his arms wide. "What's happened to my city that it exposed our sacred secret?"

"It was one of the merchants, the one who took in the last sacrifice." The messenger leaned back on his heels and rocked. He began to sweat.

"The sacrifices are for good fortune for all." Godolfin was sure his following would rise up in protest. He might even need guards if it got out of hand. "It won't go over well with the inhabitants that that merchant has given it over."

"It wasn't just that house. It is many others, and the Hebrews are still going through them. The Hebrews are relentless."

"That will cut into the fortunes of the city. My city, soon. It's time to take more daring steps."

Godolfin called in his second.

The tall angular man entered and bowed. "What is it, Prophet?"

"It is time to take the tribute. It is due about now, and the city will be less defended while the soldiers deliver the tribute to King Chedorloamer when he arrives soon. We'll make our move now."

"But this is ahead of schedule. Your army isn't fully armed yet."

"Then get them armed."

"Aye," the tall man bowed again.

"Rally the army now, we're going to take the tribute for ourselves," Godolfin ordered.

"You must realize the seriousness. That'll bring warfare down upon the city."

"Then so be it. I'll be here to pick up the city when it is over. Also get ready to arm the slaves. I'll be freeing them soon." More of his plan was unfolding and Godolfin felt his heartbeat kick up. It was time for him to take control, and he'd better be ready.

"This city is almost yours, my Lord."

"Soon," Godolfin said. "Very soon. Now, go quickly."

\*\*\*

Ashurta stared at King Birsha sitting on his elaborate carved throne. The room held the usual retinue of imperial guards and scribes, while Birsha saw to the supplicants lined up at the entrance. Ashurta challenged the king again with his stomach clenching painfully, "What is this abomination, cousin? The sacrificed babies are all over the city."

"Are they in the inner-city, too?" the king asked, fidgeting on his throne. High color rose in his face.

"We haven't gotten to the inner-city, yet. There are some victims from the inner-city, indicating access perhaps by other residents of the inner-city. It's impossible to tell who might be in collusion. The betrayals may run deep."

"You say it's this new prophet declaring the sacrifices valid?" Birsha pulled at his plaited beard, staring intently back.

"Yes, Cousin, the spies have told it." Ashurta swore under his breath. "By all that is holy, these atrocities are in the name of this prophet who's declared himself the next ruler of Gomorrah."

"What have you found out in your interrogations?"

"That he is rallying up the people to rebellion." Ashurta let out a harsh breath. "But it's hard to get the residents to talk. It's been taking dire methods. Even Ur wasn't this bad at it's worst."

"Rebellion has been a problem in this city for some time. It's nothing new." Birsha waved a hand dismissively.

"But this is a slave uprising and the middle-class is supporting it. It is evil abounding."

"That constitutes most of the city." Birsha pouted and rubbed his plaited beard.

"That's a grave concern." Ashurta had had to deal with uprisings before and the atrocities of wartime, but he'd never encountered such wickedness or forsaking of all that was good.

Birsha smoothed his plaited beard absently. "There needs to be a mass burial for the tiny victims. Their parents will be compensated from the city's coffers. That appears to be all I can do for them. This plague is too far spread in the city."

"Don't despair," Ashurta said. "My army is here to help with this problem and others like it." He knew his thousand soldiers could make a difference in peacekeeping, but he worried that it was the ingrained abominations that they couldn't keep the populace from committing. Who knew what they'd do next?

"You can't change the city," Birsha said with sadness. "I was mistaken to think that you could." He looked over Ashurta's shoulder at the line of supplicants.

"Can't I?" Ashurta thought he'd do all he could. When he'd agreed to take this post, he'd had no idea what would be entailed, nor that the city's misbehavior would be beyond reckoning.

"It is a desperate situation. Between your army of a thousand and mine of twenty we can stop some of the atrocities. But you've seen yourself how cruel the city has become."

"Cousin Lot is arriving today with his retinue. His men can help, also," Ashurta said, pacing the room.

"Yes, Lot. I've never met him. You say he is a good man?"

"He and Abraham are brave and stalwart leaders. Each has their own group now that they've divided up the grazing land and the resources."

"I should like to meet this Abraham sometime," Birsha said.

"I'm sure it can happen in the near future."

"Is he a true prophet?" Birsha raised his eyebrows.

"He walks with Jehovah, and gets inspiration direct from him." Ashurta believed in Abraham's prophesying wholeheartedly. Without him at the head of their forces, they wouldn't have made it out of Ur at its takeover; Ashurta had followed the prophet-general ever since.

"Then I should like to learn more of this Jehovah. Our god, El, is failing this city. Perhaps your god can help."

"When the searches of the houses are over, I'll meet with you again. Sometime later today when Lot has arrived. We can teach you about Jehovah then. Meanwhile, I will gather up all the infants sacrificed for a mass burial."

"Yes, that."

"Where can we bury them?"

"Use the royal mausoleum. Dig deep."

"Yes, cousin." Ashurta signaled his soldiers that waited. "Until later."

\*\*\*

Ashurta met up with Daniel on the main roadway, entering the marketplace. Ashurta sat atop his battle camel and stopped for him to approach. He was riding with more Hebrew soldiers on camels also. The animals snorted in the tepid breeze, complaining of the buzzing flies.

"Brother," Ashurta said. "I was just finishing up the rounds of the houses. Truly despicable people to have done these sacrifices."

"There won't be room for all of them in the dungeons," Daniel said. "But we can deal with them later. I've been looking for you. Lot has arrived. Turn around now. Greet cousin Lot and his men. They can help us, and they'll have news we must hear."

Ashurta raised his hand in greeting as Lot rode up from the direction of the entrance of Gomorrah along the main route. His battle camels wore armor as if he was ready for an altercation just riding into the city. Ashurta admired his readiness as he sidled closer. "I have heard dire sayings from Cousin Abraham on the road here," Lot said after his greeting.

"What does our prophet have to say?" Ashurta asked, wiping at sweat on his forehead.

Lot's face set like chiseled stone. "There is a new prophecy from angels who visited him."

"Angels?" Ashurta asked, surprised. "But angels haven't appeared to our people for centuries."

"These angels walked into his camp, and

announced the destruction of these cities of the Vale of Siddim." Lot rubbed at his clean-shaven chin, then lifted his helmet to wipe his brow.

"What kind of destruction? Surely we have enough soldiers between us within the city to fend off attackers. Plus King Chedorlaomer gets his tribute to protect this city. I'm afraid this city might destroy itself, though, before others could. You wouldn't believe how volatile it is here."

"It isn't clear how the destruction will happen," Lot answered. "But Abraham said that the angels promised that Jehovah will destroy the inhabitants for their wickedness."

"This city is an abomination," Ashurta said with understanding. "Are the other cities also this corrupt?"

"They may be even worse in Sodom," Lot complained. "I admit I've been living there now that I've separated from Abraham. My sheep graze in the hills outside the city. I had hoped for better here in Gomorrah or even one of the other cities. But I shall have to compare the two cities myself."

"That would be hard to believe," Ashurta said. "That there is a more wicked city than Gomorrah. The inhabitants are capable of unspeakable cruelties."

"Don't doubt him, brother," Daniel said.

The three cousins looked at each other for a long moment.

"What else has Abraham prophesied?" Ashurta asked.

"He has asked Jehovah to spare the cities if he can find ten righteous men within each city."

"I imagine that can be done. Then we have nothing to worry about," Ashurta said with a lift in his mood.

"I despair for Sodom," Lot said. "But I've spread the word there. The people only mocked the prophesy. I can't say I've even met ten righteous men there, myself."

Ashurta raised his arm to signal his men to ride. "We'll talk more of this later and decide what to do. Let's take you to meet our cousin, King Birsha."

"I'll follow you there with my soldiers." Lot signaled his own soldiers following behind him lining the roadway back to the gate of the city.

Ashurta urged his camel through the marketplace with the others following. They entered through the inner-city wall and came upon the palace a few minutes later.

Dismounting, they left the camels watering at a fountain and entered the palace. The guards knew Ashurta and Daniel now, so they let Lot through with his armed soldiers in tow.

The palace was dim, lit by the torches and candles strategically placed. Seated on his throne, Birsha beckoned them forward ahead of the lines of supplicants.

"Who do you have with you, Cousins?" Birsha asked.

"It is Cousin Lot, with news from Cousin Abraham," Daniel answered for them all.

Birsha rose from the throne and stepped off of the dais, crossing over to Lot. He hugged the bear of a man and thumped him on the back.

Lot pulled back and grasped forearms with the king. "I'm glad to meet you at long last."

"You are welcome here, and I see you've brought soldiers. We have need of those, too, in this city right now. You can assist your cousins while you are here."

"I've already heard there are problems in the city," Lot said.

"I will tell you of them, but come. Let's go to the dining hall and have food and drink with your men. You must be weary from your trip. The soldiers can double up in the barracks."

"They have tents. They can stay outside the city and guard it," Lot replied.

"Very well, then," Birsha said.

Birsha led the way until they were seated around the long low tables. He clapped for the servants to bring food and drink. Then he began to regale the newcomers with an account of the state of the city.

Lot grew agitated as the tales progressed. Asking for solutions to some of the problems Ashurta hadn't heard of, yet, he wondered if in fact there were even ten righteous men in this city, after all.

***

Lilliana turned as Tamru called out to her. She halted her progress across the main temple as the high priest approached.

"What is it?" she asked.

"The daily barley delivery is late."

"I wonder where Keret is?"

"The lad has been loitering around lately, and now he's late."

"I'll check the kitchen and see if they have enough for the evening meal preparations," she offered. Straightening out the sleeve on her gown, she noticed Tamru had a gleam in his eye.

"I think we should get another barley vendor to back us up," Tamru said, disgruntled.

"I don't think we need to do that yet. Keret is young but he's usually here…"

Tamru fingered his square breastplate with its jewels. "I suppose we can give him another chance."

"That's better."

"There's something else I want to talk to you about, Lilliana. Walk with me in the garden."

"I don't have much time."

"This won't take long."

"Alright." She followed him up to one of the terraced gardens.

He stopped beneath a young tree and took both her hands in his. "High priestesses and high priests have traditionally been wed before now. I don't know why it stopped, but I believe it's time to reinstate this custom."

"Tamru, you surprise me," she replied. The scent of the flowers was wafting on the warm breeze. Pulling her hands out of his, she stepped back a pace. "I don't feel we need to do that. The temple runs fine as it is."

"It's not the temple that I'm worried about. We're like an oasis amidst a desert of iniquity in this city. I think that we need to return to the old traditions to regain the favor of El and the gods and goddesses again. Our marriage would be one way to regain that trust."

"I will have to think on this thing. I will tell you my answer later." With that, she turned and left to go to the kitchen and deal with the meal preparations.

She felt overwhelmed at the prospect of changes to the temple, and didn't think she liked the idea at all of the marriage Tamru was talking about. It had been a long time since the high priest and high priestess had been required to be married. She thought they'd evolved but now Tamru suggested they were out of favor with El, their patron deity. It was true that the city had fallen into evil ways, but she doubted reinstating a marriage covenant would ally the problems. She meant what she'd told him, she'd have to think on it.

In the back of her mind, she thought of General Ashurta, her distant cousin as she made her way back down through the temple. She favored him, if she was to become eligible for marriage. He was in the royal cousinhood and suitable, and far enough away in blood to be able to marry. Plus she felt an attraction to him that she didn't feel for the high priest. If she was going to get married, she'd rather seek out Ashurta. She decided to go to the palace and see if he was there, as soon as she'd seen to the evening meal.

Keret was at the kitchen when she arrived. "Keret, where have you been?"

"I've been delayed by a meeting, High

Priestess. A meeting for the new prophet."

"Keret, you shouldn't be associating with those rebels. What has come over you?"

"I don't see what the problem is. If I can't be a scribe, then I need to do something else important. Godolfin is making many promises."

"He is a rebel who is threatening the crown. That is not how we do things in this city. We have an assembly and a king and a governor. The laws are the olden way and not to be trifled with. They come from the gods. You'd be wiser to accept your place and abide by the law."

"You're so behind the times, High Priestess. But I have to better myself. I can't always deliver barley."

"We'll talk more about this another time, Keret. Right now you need to get that barley into the kitchen. There may still be enough time before dinner."

"Right," he grumbled.

She watched him lug a bag of barley, then she took off for the palace.

She arrived without incident, but found out that her cousins were in conference together. She entered the chamber where they were having beer and bread. They turned as she entered the chamber where they sat about on plump silk cushions.

"Welcome, Sister," King Birsha said. "You may join us. We were just talking about the city." He made introductions all around and then bid her to sit next to him.

Joining them, she met her cousin Lot and his generals.

As she sat, she looked for Ashurta in the crowded room. His gaze was on her, but he was scowling. She decided to test the waters. "Great men of Gomorrah and Sodom, I have had a proposal from the high priest. He believes that if we marry that the city will become less wicked. What do you say?"

Ashurta smiled slowly at her. What was he thinking?

"I am king," Birsha stated. "I should have a say in this."

Ashurta spoke up, "I don't believe it would alleviate the city's woes from what I've seen."

"You don't believe in the power of El and Asherah?" Lilliana coughed delicately.

"I don't either," Daniel asserted.

Assent went around the room among all the Hebrews.

"What we believe in is the power of Jehovah, Lilliana," Ashurta said, standing. He paced. "Jehovah is the one supreme God and is leading our great prophet, Cousin Abraham who has been told by angels that the cities of the vale will be destroyed if ten righteous men aren't found in each city."

"How can these great cities be destroyed?" Lilliana mocked. "There aren't greater cities around, except maybe in Egypt."

"The very great will be brought to the ground," Daniel predicted.

"It can't be," Lilliana said. "But there is a greater problem than strange prophesies. There is another prophet in this city stirring up rebellion. His name is Godolfin, and his following seems to be growing by the day. His followers used to meet in secret and have oaths of secrecy, but now they grow bolder. I'm afraid Godolfin has even infiltrated the temple."

"I've heard that name from the detained prisoners over and over," Ashurta said. "They say he is the reason for the abominable sacrifices of babies that has gone on in this city. I've just uncovered it, Lilliana, and it is a city wide problem now."

"That is horrific," Lilliana gasped. "I didn't know about the practice of sacrifices. That hasn't gone on among the Kenaani for ages."

"It's back," Daniel moaned.

"Surely," King Birsha interjected. "It's been stopped now that you've discovered it."

"I hope," Ashurta said. "All the participants have been named and justice will be pursued. I regret that there are too many to keep in the dungeon with other criminals."

"How is it that this wicked prophet is practically ruling this city?" Lot asked, tugging at his beard.

"I can't say I know," King Birsha said. "I'm a good king to the people. I don't understand their rebellion."

"I've heard that he's appealing to the common man by promising to end slavery," Lilliana said.

"It is not an evil practice," King Birsha said. "It's simply an economic one. The slaves serve out their sentence, then they become one of the populace again. Simple."

"It's not simple, I'm afraid," Lilliana moued. "I hear many complaints from those who come to the temple for meals."

"I've already freed the children from becoming slaves if their parents are one," King Birsha said.

"Where is the governor?" Lot asked. "He should be here for this kind of meeting."

"Right," King Birsha said.

"I say we table this discussion until he can join us," Ashurta said.

"I want to hear more about these prophecies from Cousin Abraham," Lilliana said as she worried the hem of her purple robe.

"There's really not much more to tell," Lot said. "Abraham has been warned, and so he has told us to gather the righteous and flee the cities."

"How soon?" Daniel asked.

"That I don't know," Lot said.

"It may take time for the righteous to be gathered. They'll need time to plan," King Birsha said.

"You can't be thinking of leaving, too?" Lilliana asked.

"If the rebellion is imminent as you say, I may not have a choice," King Birsha said.

"Can't King Chedorloamer be prevailed upon to defend your throne?" Lilliana asked.

"I've just sent the tribute to him," the king said. "You may be right that there is something he can do."

"Let's pray that you are right," Ashurta said.

"We don't want to have to flee the city in a hurry. We need time to gather ourselves together. I for one will be following Abraham's orders. I don't want to leave you here alone, Cousins."

"Where will you go?" Lilliana asked.

"You'll be coming with us," Ashurta said firmly.

"There's bound to be one of the cities spared," Daniel said. "It'll only take ten righteous men from any of the cities for one to be spared."

"We don't know if one will comply yet," King Birsha said. "I wish it were Gomorrah, so we'll have to look for the ten here. It can't be that hard."

Lot scowled from across the room. "I imagine that Sodom might still have ten good men. After all, I've only just moved there."

"I had hoped to put down roots here, cousins," Ashurta said with a sad smile. "But I'll follow Abraham again as I did in Ur. He saved us then, and his prophecy will save us now."

Lot stood as Ashurta stopped pacing and sat down again. Lot said, "Let's pray together to Jehovah that he save us all, and help us find the righteous in the city."

"Hear, hear," they said. Then they all bowed their heads for a heartfelt prayer led by the king. Lilliana wondered if it would count if they could find that many righteous women. She sent her thoughts to this new deity, Jehovah. Perhaps he would be merciful.

\*\*\*

Godolfin sliced through the armor of the last soldier guarding the tribute wagons. The onlooking crowd that had followed him and his soldiers from the city gate rushed in to pull bounty off of the wagons.

Godolfin took the reins of the onagers pulling his chariot and grabbed the reins of the donkeys pulling one wagon and led it away into the depths of the city to his abode.

He left the people behind him cheering and chanting his name as they looted the wagons. His second was seated next to him and praised him loudly.

There would be another ceremony tonight, and another sacrifice to their good fortune. Soon, very soon, he could take the throne. As he unloaded the loot, he hummed contentedly to himself.

# CHAPTER EIGHT

King Birsha's general ran into the chamber. "My king, there is trouble in the city," he shouted over the conversation around the long tables where Ashurta and Lot sat with their men.

Their meeting was nearly over, and had turned to the order of business of establishing a feast to celebrate the unity with Abraham and his followers. King Birsha thought a celebration was in order, as soon as the city settled down, but Ashurta thought to himself that a celebration was premature for the very reason that the city was in upheaval. Still, he bit his words back and took a swig of beer and watched the general enter the room.

"What is it, General?" King Birsha asked. "Approach me."

"There has been an attack on the tribute wagons," the general puffed from the exertion.

"Tell me what happened?" King Birsha said, half-rising off of his cushion before sitting back down.

"Yes," the general shouted as he fell to his knees before the king. "The inhabitants have looted what the attackers left behind. The tribute is gone."

"This is terrible news," King Birsha exclaimed.

"There's more, my king. The soldiers guarding and transporting the tribute have been brutally murdered. It looks like an attack from one of the private armies."

"Then we'll have to prevail upon King Chedorlaomer" the king surmised as he rubbed his beard. "He's bound to protect us from enemies."

"These enemies are within the city," the general said.

"Enemies are enemies wherever they're found," Daniel interjected. "We'll have to kill them with or without King Chedorloamer's help."

"You're here to put order back into the city," the king said. "Not cause a rebellion as would happen if you attack the local citizenry."

"Even if they're looting the tribute?" Daniel quirked an eyebrow.

"That's enough," Ashurta said. "The liege king will have to do his duty and help the City of Gomorrah."

"What can he do if you can't control the city?" the general asked Ashurta directly.

"I have more help now with Cousin Lot and his soldiers arriving," Ashurta replied.

"I'm afraid for you, my king. The looting isn't stopping with the tribute," the general said.

"What else is happening?" Birsha asked,

bent forward.

The general kneeled closer to the seated king. "The looting is being carried out in the middle quadrant. It'll soon be up here in the inner-city."

"Cousins," King Birsha turned to the assembled company. "What do you have to say? Are you prepared as you've said for the defense of the city and my person?"

"What do you need from us?" Ashurta and Lot asked at the same time.

"The city is being overrun by looters. I need you to stop them," the king determined. "General, take soldiers to the dividing line between the quadrants and set up a line of defense for the inner-city. Ashurta, and Lot, take your forces to the inner-city and the front gate."

"This may be the start to a full-scale rebellion," Daniel surmised aloud, pushing back from the low table.

"It may be," Ashurta agreed. "We can stop this with action now. But we have to move on it right away."

"That is what I think has to happen now," King Birsha said. "Go with your soldiers and mine to stop the rebellion from growing. I'll join you shortly at the inner-city gate."

"My men are armed," Lot said. "I will report in from the front gate as soon as we put down the rebellion there."

"Very good. We should have this rebellion under control in no time," King Birsha said and rose to go don his armor. "Make haste. Ashurta, I've thought of something. The marketplace will need help. Go there, first, before withdrawing to the inner-city. I'll meet you there."

Ashurta's blood pumped with fury as he left to do the king's bidding. Memories of the rebellion in Ur and his failure to put it down sluiced over him like bile. Still, he loped off to gather his soldiers for the bitter task at hand. He wouldn't fail this time.

*\*\*\**

The marketplace was filled with people running to and fro, some with wares under their arms. Ashurta couldn't tell who was a merchant and who was a looter as he sat atop one of the king's horses in full armor. Screams were filling the street and some fires were raging at the merchant wagons in one area.

He wished he'd gotten to know the merchants so he'd know who to help, but he'd been occupied by the investigation into the sacrifices. Now he noted that merchants' wagons and carts were set up before houses where the merchants were escaping into with their wares. Some of them were being followed by looters fighting them for what they carried in their arms.

Some wagons had overturned. Here and there, someone lay on the ground, having been beaten down.

Ashurta decided to help the merchants still struggling to reach the safety of their houses. He barked orders to his soldiers over the din. Immediately his soldiers began assisting the merchants.

He turned to Lot riding a battle camel next to him. "Take the quarter near the entrance to the city now. There may be some of King Birsha's soldiers still there. Prevent the looters from fleeing the city."

"I will," Lot said. He took off at a good clip with his own soldiers intent to reach the entrance.

Ashurta spotted a woman with a baby strapped to her body struggling to pull swaths of fine cloth out of the hands of a looter.

He dismounted ran to her side and drew his sword, holding the tip at the neckline of the looter, pushing into the beard. "Back away, or I'll kill you."

"Thank you, Hebrew," the woman panted, clutching the cloth, and shielding her baby.

The looter sidestepped and took off running.

"How did you know I'm a Hebrew?" He cocked an eyebrow.

"Your accent. I've served many of the Hebrews since you've been here."

"Let's get your wares into your house and then you can bar the doors and windows."

She grabbed more cloth and he did the same, following her into the spacious two-story house. After more such trips, they stood at the doorway. The melee outside was beginning to move off in another direction, Ashurta noted. He'd have to pursue it with his men.

"Mistress, bar your doors and windows behind me."

"But I'm watching for my husband," she said. "He must get back soon."

"He'll want you to be safe. Quickly, now."

Ashurta stepped outside and heard the resounding evidence of the bar being dropped into place.

He withdrew his sword again, and chased away more looters as his men were gathering in the middle of the street. Looking about, he noted with satisfaction that the street was now all but deserted except for soldiers. His men were making short work of it. This was better than Ur.

Daniel stepped forward, blood evident on his drawn sword. "The looters are moving up toward the inner-city."

"First," Ashurta said. "Is everyone accounted for?" He looked around at the faces of his men and went in order of rank, calling them out. Once everyone had checked in some minutes later, he said, "Alright, let's go up to the inner-city now."

They marched and rode as a cohesive unit uphill to the gate of the inner-city. Crowds of looters were already running from house to house. The air was punctuated by screams of fear and outrage. Battles were happening in the street and in the houses.

"Take both sides of the streets," Ashurta barked the order.

"He took the first house on his right and pushed the door open without knocking. Inside, he found a luxurious setting marred with blood spray about the room. He searched further and found a dead man. The man had had his throat slashed. As Ashurta looked around the place, it looked like from the patterns of dust that several items had been taken from the shelves. In this quadrant, it was likely luxury items. The inner-city was extremely wealthy. This bode ill for the inhabitants. The looting had turned deadly.

He searched the rest of the house, calling out for anyone that might be hiding. No answer came.

He exited onto the street and ran up it looking for the next house that his men weren't already inside. He loped around the corner turning east and heading towards the palace as the thought occurred to him to check on King Birsha.

He took off at a full run up the hill.

He panted to a halt at the entrance to the palace where two guards held ground.

"Guards," Ashurta said to the two armed imperial guards at the grand palace entrance. "Where is your king?"

"He has gone out to defend the city," the one on the right explained. "He is in full armor and ready for battle. He has his guards with him."

"Which direction did he go?" Ashurta had a clenching in his gut at the thought of the king going out into battle and endangering his own life. But kings had been at the front of battles for eons since the days of living in caves when the king was the first one to rush out and defend the tribe and only recently had many of the kings refused to go out and fight at all. King Birsha was simply following the ancient ways.

"He went north toward the gateway. He wanted to hold off the rebellion at the wall," the same guard explained.

Ashurta spit onto the ground, then looked

the guards over as if to assess them for their battle readiness. "The rebellion has grown deadly. There are already dead residents in the inner-city. Man the palace doors with your lives."

"Aye," the guards echoed, both snapping to attention at Ashurta's commanding presence.

Ashurta turned on his heel and ran off toward the gate where he'd just come from. Once there, he searched for the king and found him ordering the inner-city gates closed.

Ashurta looked out into the rest of the city and saw a horror. The king pointed to an advancing army reaching the marketplace. Their black banners sporting white snakes announced their arrival. Riding into the city in chariots drawn by onagers and with foot-soldiers marching behind them, the army could be seen extending all the way out to the entrance of the city.

A pit fisted itself in Ashurta's center. Who was attacking the city already in rebellion?

"Those are King Chedorloamer's soldiers arriving," King Birsha exclaimed to Ashurta while his guards shut the inner gate. "They told my scout that they were going to put down the rebellion and take their tribute out of the city. I don't understand it, but the tribute I sent him disappeared. King Chedorloamer is furious apparently and won't see reason. I sent a messenger with a conciliatory message but he returned with the bad news."

"Our best defense then is to close up the inner-city and wait him out," Ashurta replied. "We don't have enough men to take on the king's army and the citywide looters, as well."

Daniel came bounding up, hearing the last. "It'll be all we can do to take back this part of the city."

"Kill all the looters," King Birsha ordered. "Pass the order along."

Daniel looked to Ashurta as he said, "I'm afraid it'll have to be done. I've already found dead in their homes. Stop the rebellion any way that you can."

"I will tell the men," Daniel said and then turned on his heel and ran back toward the melee.

"Ashurta," King Birsha said, stroking blood on his armor, a forlorn expression creasing his brow. "I'm afraid I may've lost my city."

"Cousin," Ashurta gasped as he peered closer at the blood on the king's armor. "Are you injured?"

"It's nothing. I can still fight on. Don't try to dissuade me."

"Then I will fight by your side today. I won't leave you." Ashurta had a sudden thought. "What of cousin Lot and his soldiers? They were at the entrance to the city."

"I don't know about their whereabouts, but you'll want to pray to your Jehovah for him since I've never seen the city like this before. I already tried praying to El, but he isn't hearing my pleas this day."

"I will do that," Ashurta said, pivoting to survey the scene around them. Hebrew soldiers were herding back a group of infiltrating looters towards the end of the street, rounding them up. Ashurta jogged up to the soldiers and commanded them, "The king has ordered all looters killed for their treasonous acts here. Follow my lead."

With that, he stabbed the nearest looter in the gut. The others who were still clutching armsful of luxury items dropped them with a clatter and tried to run off in any which direction. The Hebrews gave chase and Ashurta returned to the king's side, confident his men could get to all the looters with the help of the king's own men.

He reported in to the king what had transpired and the king saluted him back, calling him his general. They made their way away from the gateway and King Birsha sent Ashurta down an alleyway where a scuffle was happening. The guards followed the king around to the front of the building.

Ashurta looked down the alleyway and saw a small group of looters beating one of the inner-city residents judging by his fine robe. Swinging his sword into the air, and lifting his shield, he rammed into the back of one of the attackers. Three more stepped back, wary of his sword arm as they danced sideways.

Remembering the king's order to kill the looters, Ashurta sliced the head off of the nearest looter. The other three turned around and fled. Ashurta put up a chase and caught the older and slower man from behind. Another head removed.

He took off after the other two again, but they split at the next street, fleeing in different directions. One was running further into the inner-city depths, and the other one was running toward the gate. Figuring the king's guards at the gate would cut down that man, he quickly trailed the other one. There was another alleyway, and the looter turned into it.

Ashurta burst around the corner, only to find that the looter was gaining ground and heading towards the next street. Pushing himself faster and feeling the sweat slide off of his hairline under his helmet, Ashurta chased the looter.

At the intersection, the looter turned deeper again and this time when Ashurta turned the corner, he couldn't see him. Scanning the street, he noted all the doors were closed.

He went to the first door on the left and pounded. No answer came so he pushed open the door and found a woman and small boy huddled inside. She was shivering profoundly and the two of them each held a kitchen knife.

"Mistress, did a man come in here just now?" Ashurta barked.

She shook her head. He turned back to the door and noticed it didn't have a bar. This inner-city had been a safer place before today.

"Mistress, when I'm gone, push your furniture in front of the door to bar it from the attackers."

She quivered, but nodded assent.

He bound back out to the street, and saw the looter running again, this time toward the city gate. He gave chase, cursing his legs for not going faster.

As the gate neared, he saw that it was unguarded and someone had opened it. Where were the guards that had been posted?

The looter ran out the gate and into the fray

of the army sacking the city.

Ashurta stopped at the gate and pulled it closed again, dropping the large bar across it with an effort that would've normally have taken two men.

He stopped and removed his helmet and swiped away the sweat before putting it back on.

Where was the king now?

He could hear the sound of battle outside the gate, and also from further inside the compound. Making his way toward the noise, he glanced down each alleyway as he marched uphill.

In one alley, he found a guard from the palace in the blue uniform. He was lolling on the ground with a wound in his side.

"Good man, what has happened to you? You're not at the palace."

"I … I have fought the king's attackers but they got me."

"I'll get you help, but tell me which way the king went."

"The fight moved up the alley and onto that second street," the guard heaved. "I don't know from there."

"Wait here, and you'll be helped," Ashurta reassured.

"I can still defend myself," the guard lifted the sword at his side valiantly.

Ashurta ran down the alley and past the first street intersection. Looking both directions, he saw no sign. Proceeding to the second street, he found the sprawled bodies of two more guards.

He checked them. Both dead. Where was the

king?

The howl of a victory cry emitted from around the next corner. Ashurta followed it to the scene of the king laid out face down on the ground with a pool of blood spanning out.

He looked up the alleyway and saw a golden-haired giant of a man running with other armed men. He didn't recognize him for one of the leaders in the city or the uniforms they were wearing.

"King Birsha!" Kneeling beside the king, he noted that two more guards appeared dead nearby.

He turned the king over and found the deep thrusting wound in his chest. Blood spurted out of it, and stained Ashurta's uniform.

"Birsha, Birsha," Ashurta took his cousin in his arms. "Can you hear me?"

Opening his eyes, Birsha squinted in pain. "Stop him," he gurgled.

"Who did this to you?"

"Prophet … Godolf—"

The king's head rolled to the side and he went still.

Ashurta yelled his rage, raising his face to the bright sky.

Then he stood and hefted the king over his shoulder and began the short trek back to the palace. Once there, he shouted orders at the guards and carried the king to his rooms and laid him on the bed.

After a few minutes, the court physician ran in, carrying a basket of tools and cloth and herbs. But when he checked the king, he declared him dead.

Ashurta hung his head as palpable pain swept through him. His muscles tensed under the sudden strain of it all.

Ashurta suddenly remembered the injured guard lying in the alleyway. He told two of the imperial guards where he was and they departed to retrieve him.

Ashurta turned back to the king and knelt by his bed on one knee. He removed the king's helmet and stroked back his soaked hair. He despaired that he'd been unable to protect the king, but now he knew who to pursue.

Godolfin was in the inner-city and he had to find him before he escaped.

\*\*\*

Lilliana clung to the walls as she made her way to the palace. She'd entered while the gate was still open but was strangely unguarded. Behind her, an army was entering the city and she knew she had to get to the palace. All around chaos erupted. As she'd run by many establishments, she observed bloodshed. The whole city seemed to be bathed in a deafening outcry.

As she turned a corner, she came face to face with a large blonde man with a crooked nose and eagle-sharp eyes. He was massively strong and in elegant attire, wielding a bloodied sword. He pinned her with his gaze and she felt her knees weaken in panic.

He laughed when he saw her.

The small army of men with him were in red uniforms and fine armor and their weapons also bore signs of use.

Which side of the fray were they on?

The blonde man stepped closer.

She recoiled. She didn't know who he was, but the light of madness was in his eyes.

"Come join me, High Priestess," he quipped.

Her heart sunk as awareness began dawning on her. "I don't know who you are," she sputtered, backing against the wall as the soldiers began to surround her. She couldn't escape now, and would have to face down their leader.

"I'm the rightful ruler of this city now." His gaze shifted over her strangely. "You may as well know it and accept it."

She fell back a pace. "I don't know what you're talking about." She hoped to dissuade him and to slide away along the wall. She took a tentative step, letting the air in her lungs out in a whoosh.

"Don't argue with me," he warned, his eyebrows meeting in a scowl. He took a step to follow her short movement.

Straightening to her full height, she wondered if she could dash between the surrounding soldiers. She wished she'd brought a weapon but all she had was her knife. Not much effect against this many men, but she reached for it anyhow. Weilding it in front of her, she noted with satisfaction that the soldiers stepped back with a healthy respect.

"You can't escape, High Priestess." He

scowled.

"Let me pass," she demanded, inhaling deeply. She felt her heart pummeling in her chest and real dread seeped into her consciousness.

"I can't do that," he said. "Not now that we've met."

"I want no trouble with you and your men."

"Join me, and I will make you my queen." Now he was smiling.

"What?" she gasped. "You're not a member of the royalty."

"Ah, but I am," he chortled under his breath. Smiles appeared on the faces of the men around.

A few laughed, causing goosebumps along the nape of her neck.

She had known all the royal cousinhood and the nobles in the city, and most had their own private armies and ran quadrants of the city which suited King Birsha and the governor just fine. With a growing sense of desperation as the soldiers' initial fear of her knife hand waned, she asked, "where are you a king that you'd suppose I'd be your queen?"

"How is it that you don't know who I am?" he asked audaciously.

"I don't know who you are," she said with as much courage as she could muster. She wouldn't give him the satisfaction. "But I won't help you with treason against this king. You must be with King Chedorloamer out there in the main city."

Blood was dripping off of his sword and some of the others. She quivered and shuffled her feet, ready to bolt.

"Your brother is dead, and I'm the next in line to rule," he announced in a surly voice.

"King Chedorloamer is taking control of the city now. I can't say that I approve of his methods, but he is the liege here. He'll make you pay," she stated with more courage than she felt.

His smile grew broad. "I am king here now. King Chedorloamer will retreat soon, mark me."

"Now I know who you are. You're that false prophet, Godolfin. I won't help you."

"Oh, but you will."

"I won't." She lifted the knife menacingly. "Besides, I couldn't become queen with you."

"You think you can be queen now on your own?" He guffawed and threw his head back in emphasis, mocking her. A guttural sound escaped him.

"I want to know what you've done to King Birsha. He is a good king, and the city will follow him again –"

"The city won't be following him anymore for I have killed him."

"Killed him?" She felt blood drain from her head and she wondered if she'd faint. "Even if it's true—"

"It's the truth," he growled. "It doesn't matter if you believe me now. You'll soon see."

"I won't help you. You're an imposter to the throne."

"I'm the next in line, along with you."

"I don't believe you."

"It had to come to this, and you will see reason in time. Now, marry me and we'll rule together."

"What gives you a right to rule?" She hesitated asking the question, afraid of the answer.

"I'm Birsha's bastard brother. Your father didn't remain faithful and now I will rule. Come, we'll be married in the old tradition and rule of the gods."

"You can't be serious. That old rule was abolished, besides it was for siblings with the same mother but different fathers. Only Egypt sometimes still practices it. You and I have different mothers, so it wouldn't have qualified."

"Don't argue with me," he growled. "You will come with me now even if it isn't willingly. You are of the bloodline of the goddess. Therefore I will drink your moonblood for long life like our ancestors. And we will marry as the gods proclaimed. I'll restore the old ways now."

"You're not only a false prophet, you're a madman!" she screeched, backing up along the wall away from him and turning to run. Gathering her courage, she made a mad dash.

"Take her!" Godolfin shouted to his soldiers.

# CHAPTER NINE

Imperial guards were running about delivering the news that the king had fallen. Their blue uniforms were soaked in sweat from the exertions of the battles and the effort of trying to maintain order within the palace grounds.

"It was fought valiantly," Ashurta stated to the governor Yassib who'd arrived at the city gates a few minutes ago with news that Chedorloamer and his army were leaving the city. They stood in the throne room with more Hebrews and the governor's soldiers.

"The question of who is in charge needs to be answered now before more chaos erupts," Yassib said. "I can't run this city by myself. Especially not now that it has turned violent all over."

Daniel cleared his throat as he stepped up to the pair near the throne. "King Birsha didn't have an heir."

"I run many of the functions of the city,"

Yassib said. "But the people look to the king. If I fall, there would simply be another governor elected from among the people. But a kingship is inherited. It's essential that the people have a true king to follow. Now more than ever. With that false prophet trying to get the whole city to follow him, we need a strong leader now. Someone to bring the city out of its current path of destruction."

Ashurta scuffed his heel on the stonework. "I'm the next in line, then, from the bloodlines present. I can take over until the other kings of the sister cities can offer to run Gomorrah. I think that in the long run, that'll be best. I have the royal blood so that should be enough for the people." He shuffled his feet, feeling uncomfortable with the new weight of responsibility that he was volunteering for. He added, "for now."

"I think that is a great idea," Yassib exclaimed.

"We just need the high priest to install you," Daniel said.

"Speaking of the high priest and high priestess, has anyone seen them today?" Ashurta called out to the throng watching him with his brother and the governor.

"The high priestess is within the inner-city today," one of the soldiers stated. "I saw her a little while ago."

"I'd hoped that those two were being protected at the temple by their own guards and mine while we were in battle today. I should've gone over there myself but I didn't want to leave the king's side." Regret washed over Ashurta as he surveyed his battle weary men, most of them covered in unsavory grime. They'd been a victorious lot, so he attempted a smile to reassure them as they watched him.

"The high priest is a trained fighter, and so is the high priestess," the governor reassured. "I'm sure they fared well during the uprising. After all, she defeated my own son who was well trained for combat."

"I'll go to the temple now and fetch the high priest for this impromptu installation," Daniel volunteered, stepping forward.

"Be careful. The city is still in some chaos," Yassib said. "King Chedorlaomer has taken many hostages and all the bounty his army can carry, which is quite a lot I can tell you."

"I will be swift about it," Daniel said.

"Take the imperial guards with you," Ashurta decided. "They're fresh and not battle weary like our Hebrew soldiers."

"Guards," Daniel called out. Gathering the remainder, he told them the planned route to the temple along some side roads and less frequented alleys he knew of.

Overhearing, the governor interjected, "There's a tunnel to the temple from the palace.

"Show us where it is," Daniel requested. "If it's clear, we'll take it."

"Daniel," Ashurta said. "Also find out where Lot is and his army. They were thick in the fray the last we heard."

"If I don't find his whereabouts while on my errand, I'll go back out and search for him."

"He was at the city's main gate when King Chedorlaomer arrived," one of the soldiers piped in.

"Then that's where I'll look," Daniel said. He walked quickly to the palace entrance.

"Hurry. Follow me," Yassib said.

The governor led the way through the palace.

Ashurta's men filtered throughout the palace to guard it, and now him that he was being crowned king, even if temporarily. Ashurta stood in front of the carved throne and offered up a silent prayer to Jehovah that Gomorrah wouldn't turn out like Ur.

***

It wasn't more than an hour later that the rush coronation took place.

The high priest hurriedly anointed Ashurta with olive oil and recited a plaintive prayer to El to accept the new king as his own.

Ashurta followed up the prayer with one of his own to Jehovah, imploring him to guide him in his new role.

Ashurta accepted the crown on his head and addressed his gathered soldiers. As he encouraged them in a speech, he wondered in the back of his mind where Lilliana was. He'd sent out soldiers to look for her in the inner-city after Daniel had gone on his errand. He hoped she was safe and simply tending to her flock. She was royal, too, and should be here helping him run the city. She knew it best with the exception of the governor. As he closed his speech to a rousing cry from his men, he called two of them up.

"Brodin and Evber," Ashurta said. "Go out into the city and search for the high priestess. She wasn't at the temple when Daniel fetched the high priest, and I'm concerned."

"Right away," Brodin offered.

"Aye," Evber said. "But we should have more men with us as it's getting dark. After we were taken by the city inhabitants last time, I don't want a repeat of that cage experience."

"Take more soldiers then," Ashurta assigned four more soldiers and sent them on their way.

He removed the crown carefully from his head and walked over to the throne and placed the crown on it. Feeling as though it was only a temporary situation, he didn't want to get too used to it. Already, the mantle of responsibility of ruling was beginning to weigh heavily on him.

***

"High Priestess Lilliana has been kidnapped," Evber said. He was distraught with the news he bore.

Ashurta flared, rising from the table where he sat in the kitchen refreshing himself. "Where is she?"

"Godolfin the prophet has her."

"How do I find this Godolfin?" Ashurta asked.

"He is making no secret of his whereabouts," Evber said.

"Then let's go get her," Ashurta said.

"There's more …" Evber said.

"What else do you have to tell me? Speak up."

"Godolfin has declared himself the ruler of Gomorrah."

"Has he now?" Ashurta rubbed his chin thoughtfully. Then he called out for the soldiers to gather in the throne room. When they'd filed in, he ordered two of them, "find Governor Yassib. He may be in danger from Godolfin who is trying to take over the city. You, and you," Ashurta pointed to two soldiers. "Go find him. The rest of you I want with me to go get High Priestess Lilliana from Godolfin's clutches. Form up now."

Gathering their weapons, they set out to find Godolfin in the inner workings of the city on the royal horses. The sound of the hooves thundered along the hard-packed main road.

While enroute down through the marketplace, a soldier riding in from the main gate stopped Ashurta. "General," the rider said. "The news is bad about Lot. He and his army have been taken captive by King Chedorloamer."

"That is bad news," Ashurta said. "We shall have to go rescue him."

"But how can we?" Daniel said from behind him, pushing his way to the front on his horse which neighed with the excitement in the air. "We have to go get Lilliana, too."

"We will have to get Lilliana now, and you go get Lot. Notify Abraham, Daniel. He'll lead his army against Chedorloamer with us. Take most of the soldiers with you. You'll need them."

"Right. I'll leave now for Abraham's pastures. He may have allies, too, that we can call upon."

Ashurta notified his lieutenants about the change in plans. Word passed along the line.

Daniel turned his horse toward the city's main gate and rode off with the soldiers following in formation Ashurta watched them until the dust from their passing settled.

"Now, let's go get the high priestess," Ashurta ordered the few remaining Hebrews.

They went to the place that Evber had said Godolfin was holed up in the east-side of the city, but the house was deserted. Ashurta sent soldiers to inquire of the neighbors. It appeared in fact that all the neighboring houses were also empty.

Dismounting, the soldiers began going door to door further along looking for him or his followers. The city residents were reluctant to give up Godolfin until they learned that Ashurta was the new king. Then some few of them became helpful.

"He is in the caves above the city," one man said from his doorway, bowing to Ashurta.

"Where?" the soldier questioning him asked.

"The ceremonial cave is up there," the man pointed to the northwest hillside. "It's not far."

"How do you get there?" Ashurta asked, suspicious of the talk of a ceremony. He already knew about the infant sacrifices that Godolfin had been conducting. His gut was telling him to hurry. "Is there a shortcut there?"

"There is a tunnel the followers take up there at night. It goes from the houses on the south side of the city."

"That's the impoverished neighborhood," Ashurta said. "Let's go."

The soldiers mounted up again and followed Ashurta into the south of the city near the main gate. He stopped at the first house and banged on the door. The unhappy couple that answered the door grew shocked when Ashurta demanded access to the tunnel.

"We don't have a tunnel here, general," the man at the door said.

"Hurry, do it now," Ashurta insisted. "There is no time to waste. Open the tunnel now or I'll put you in the dungeon."

The quivering man stepped back and went to the back door and out into the yard where the family mausoleum led downward below ground level. He backed up into the mausoleum with his hands held high.

"You don't want to go in there, general."

"Give me your torches over there and go light them for me," Ashurta ordered.

Scurrying away with the unlit torches, the man cast a fearful look over his shoulder.

By the time he returned, Ashurta had divided the soldiers up again. Some were going with him through the tunnel to fight their way in that way, and the rest would go out the city gate and ride up into the foothills to the caves, looking for the entrance that way. They'd meet up in battle again.

Ashurta grabbed the torches and handed one to the soldier who'd taken up the rear. He told the owner of the house to open the tunnel door. The man pushed aside a tall wooden shelf and a doorway loomed.

"Good. Follow me," Ashurta said.

His soldiers filed into the tunnel behind him.

The first curve of the tunnel was followed by a straight path. It was short in height a little so Ashurta had to stoop but he pushed ahead as fast as he could. The tunnel was braced up by wooden beams, and the torchlight flickered off shadowy crevices where scuttling sounds were heard.

Dust rose up around them, and Ashurta coughed. After a quarter of an hour, noise ahead could be heard and Ashurta slowed the group to a cautious pace. He planned to meet up with the other contingent arriving at the cave entrance. He hoped they'd find the right cave in time.

Easing up to the opening of a chamber, he passed the word back along the ranks that it was time to charge in.

Silhouettes of men could be seen at the exit of the tunnel across the chamber. They appeared to be guarding the cave entrance. From where he stood in the darkness of the tunnel, Ashurta could see the prophet on a raised platform at the head of a large crowd. He heard him calling out his treasonous orders.

An inner fire rose up inside Ashurta as he withdrew his weapon and moved forward.

With a deft slice of his sword, he cut down the first man, and turned to stab the next one.

He stepped into the dim cavern. It was crowded with people all facing a central altar and the large blonde man holding up a baby now.

Next to him, Lilliana was bound by the hands, but she kicked out at the prophet, and he turned and slapped her hard. She fell to the ground.

In the seconds that it took, Ashurta rushed into the cavern with his soldiers fanning out, slicing and hacking as they went.

Cries of fear and of outrage went up and the crowd began to fall back. As the soldiers were filling the cavern, the crowd pushed out the entrance to head down the hillside while emitting fearful cries into the engulfing night.

Ashurta glanced at the prophet and saw that he was springing around the altar and withdrawing his own sword.

The torchlight glinted off of the weapons in play. Bloodcurdling screams filled the air as the massacre progressed.

Ashurta turned in time to parry the prophet's sword.

The clash reverberated down his arm at the prophet's strength.

Around them, the prophet's soldiers in red uniforms had moved to engage the Hebrew soldiers.

Ashurta heard the Hebrew war cry from the front of the cave. The crowd was trapped.

The soldiers fought, and Ashurta concentrated on his own battle with the bigger man.

They fought on, and Ashurta felt fresh energy fill him, despite the prophet's expertise in battle. The big man fell suddenly, and Ashurta jumped back to assess the situation.

Behind the prophet, Lilliana stood, still

bound. She'd thrown herself at the prophet and now teetered and fell as the crush of fighting men pushed in around her.

Her gaze locked with Ashurta's and he felt his hearbeat thud stronger. He stepped around the scrambling prophet to pull Lilliana back onto her feet and prevent her from being trampled.

As he did so, two pairs of fighters crashed into her again and she was thrown into his arms. He caught her, and held her close for a breath, then led her through the battle to the tunnel opening.

"Give me your ropes," Ashurta said.

"Hurry," she said and turned for him to slice through the ropes tying her wrists.

"The baby, is it alive?" Ashurta asked.

"No, it was sacrificed by impalement like the others of the city. Godolfin is pure evil."

Speaking of Godolfin, Ashurta looked about for the prophet and could see him nowhere. "Do you see him?"

"No. But look, the people are escaping through the entrance and another tunnel behind the altar."

Swearing under his breath, Ashurta propelled her into the tunnel he'd taken to await the outcome.

Returning to the cave, he noted many dead fallen from both armies. His own soldiers were carrying wounded outside the cave. He made his way to the entrance and surveyed the scene. A group of citizens had been rounded up and were being held by Hebrew soldiers. The injured were being laid out on the other side of the entrance.

From down in the valley, he could hear random cries and thought he could see by the moonlight the forms of men and women rushing away.

Returning to the cave, Ashurta searched the perimeter and found four more tunnels leading out of the cavern. The last of Godolfin's remaining army still fighting were being disarmed or killed, and suddenly the cave became quiet.

Ashurta didn't know which tunnel Godolfin and his army had retreated into, so he found Lilliana again and asked her what she'd seen.

"I saw them go into two tunnels. I didn't see which one the prophet went into."

Retrieving torches from the walls, Ashurta singled out two of his soldiers. "Run along the tunnels over there and there and seek signs of the retreating army. Especially that prophet."

The soldiers took off scrambling into the low tunnels.

Ashurta turned back to Lilliana. "Are you hurt in any way?"

"I bear bruises but little more," she said. "Godolfin didn't have time to act on his threats."

"What threats?"

"Oh, a few, including forcing me into marriage."

"Marriage?" Ashurta was aghast.

"He is insane. He thinks he's the new king. He claims he killed King Birsha and that he's a half-brother with a claim to the throne."

"That explain a lot," Ashurta said. "Let's get you back to the palace now.

He took her hand and led her out into the night, the torchlight dancing on the hillside as they climbed down.

Here and there they stepped over the fallen. Their eyes grew accustomed to the darkness as they made their way down the hillside.

When they approached the city, it was full of activity and people out and about. As Ashurta rode with Lilliana back to the palace, he kept his bloodied sword withdrawn to deter any attackers.

No one challenged him when they saw them, but he didn't know how long that would last so he pushed the horse they'd retrieved on faster.

As they arrived, the palace appeared deserted, and Ashurta found a couple of looters running out with their arms full of treasures.

"Wait here," he barked.

He ran after the closest bandit and felled him with one swing. The treasures clacked onto the roadway.

He looked for the other looter and saw him too far ahead to catch up to so he returned to Lilliana's side. "Let's go inside. The soldiers will be back soon with the new prisoners."

"They will find more resistance as they enter the city again."

"That may be, but let's get you cared for first. Then we'll go check on the temple once the soldiers are back."

Lilliana borrowed a robe from her dead brother, a resplendent white one with gold embroidery to replace her soiled one.

Finding Ashurta outside the door where

she'd changed, she asked, "Are you ready to go back to the temple now?"

"Let's wait for some soldiers to return and then we'll go with some of them."

"Do you think the rioting will happen again?"

"If it's anything like Ur was when it fell, then yes, I do." He scowled, fearing what would happen from the city being in chaos. He again felt the loss of Ur and his failure there. He wondered if he could restore order to Gomorrah and lead it, after all. His mind swam in his doubts.

"Then let's see if there is any food in the kitchen, or maybe some servants left in the palace somewhere," Lilliana said plaintively. "I haven't eaten since yesterday, and I'd like to know if the servants have stayed."

"I'll follow you." Ashurta tried to smile reassuringly at Lilliana, but wondered if he could keep her safe with Godolfin on the loose. He placed his hand in the small of her back and propelled her carefully forward to the kitchen, wondering how long the palace would be his home. And how long taming Gomorrah would take.

*** 

Soldiers were returning with prisoners in tow that they herded through the main entrance into the large hall before they were put into the dungeon. A soldier was acting as scribe as none of the servants had been found, cataloging the captured citizens and occasional soldier of Godolfin.

Lilliana recognized some of the prisoners from better times at the temple. She spotted Neanna, the fine fabric merchant woman among them. Pushing forward through the soldiers, Lilliana reached out and got Neanna's attention. Her head lifted.

"Neanna," Lilliana said. "I'm surprised to see you here."

"I've been caught when I was trying to help my husband get his freedom."

"But that false prophet is trouble. You shouldn't believe him. We at the temple have always been good to you. You should've come to me for help."

"He's a true prophet, and I know he'll free the slaves if he hasn't already."

"He must be behind the city riots." Lilliana longed to convince everyone following Godolfin of the folly in it. "He's very dangerous."

"He's the new ruler of Gomorrah whether you or anyone likes it or not," Neanna said, her eyes glittering.

"Where is your baby boy?"

A strange look came over her and she threw back her head. "I gave him up for Godolfin to appease the gods."

"Neanna, that was your baby he sacrificed?"

"So that my husband can be free. It'll please the gods and free the slaves and bless everyone with abundance."

"Neanna, that's horrible. Those sacrifices were outlawed long ago and I can't believe you took part," Lilliana gasped at the shock of it all.

"I can't explain it to you, but it is the best way to follow the prophet. You just don't understand what he can do."

Lilliana frowned, feeling a strange tingle over her spine. Godolfin was still out there, somewhere, in Gomorrah. Perhaps gathering more followers with his tricks and deceit. She felt responsible as a high priestess for the city's occupants and their beliefs. She'd fulfilled her job the best that she could, but now there was obviously doubt and confusion about the old gods and goddesses. Perhaps they'd truly abandoned the city and its people. Perhaps the Hebrews new god was better for them all. He seemed to be a just god from what she'd learned. She decided to ask Ashurta more about him and his ways.

She addressed Neanna again before the guards took her away. "There is another prophet predicting the end to this city. You must've heard by now."

"This city can't be destroyed," Neanna said. "The prophet has promised the city will thrive again. Like in the olden times. We just have to be faithful to the return of the old ways that he's started."

"It will be destroyed. I know this new prophet of the Hebrews is correct. His God is speaking to my heart. He is a new deity for us. Jehovah is what he's called. You should abandon Godolfin and embrace this new better god."

"I only know that Godolfin has been fulfilling his promises. He'll free me, you'll see."

"You've fallen prey to this foolishness,

Neanna. I can see that there is nothing I can do for you now so I shall pray for your soul." Still horrified, Lilliana signaled the soldiers they could move their prisoners along.

The soldiers herded the prisoners to the dungeon, and Lilliana was left feeling discouraged at Neanna's sacrifice. How could the people be fooled by Godolfin? The man was pure evil, even if he was a royal. Her brother had been a good king, and now his influence seemed to have been in vain. He had truly loved Gomorrah and devoted his life to it. Now what would become of Gomorrah? Their cousin Abraham had prophesied its demise due to evil ways. She admitted she was having a hard time finding much good left in the city.

Still, it was her home and she felt conflicted. If only she could do something. It seemed their only hopes relied upon King Ashurta now. King. If the city would accept him and follow his just ways. Where was he?

She searched for Ashurta in the palace and found him still in the kitchens securing food for his returning men. He was cooking soup over the fire he'd built in the oven. He'd laid out bread on the fine plates the palace boasted of. She was touched to see him caring for his men in such a way, and she decided to help him.

She carried platters of bread into the dining hall where they'd celebrated the feasts such a short time ago. Then she carried out bowls of soup and placed them in front of the waiting soldiers who hadn't had a chance yet to clean up after battle in more than a cursory manner.

It took hours to feed all the soldiers who took shifts. When the last group had eaten their fill of dates for dessert, Lilliana asked Ashurta if they could go to the temple.

"We need to prepare to leave this city," Ashurta sitting next to her told her close to her ear.

She felt a shiver at his breath. Looking closely at him, she asked, "do we have a choice?"

"The soldiers will get us out safely."

"I'm sure they could. But what of Cousin Abraham's prophesy? What do I do about this situation?" His gaze was riveting her, and she wondered deep down if there was some special future for them together. Whatever would happen, it was clear that they had to get out of the troubles they were in at the moment before they could find out. She sighed.

"You can make your preparations if you do it quickly at the temple."

"How much time do I have?"

"Time is short. You have until tomorrow morning to plan, unless I find the ten righteous men here, that is."

"Do you really think Cousin Abraham's prophecy will come true?" she asked, shaken even more at the thought of it. "How could this great city be destroyed?"

"Abraham heard it from angels, face to face, so it's bound to be true."

"It's just so hard to accept. So hard to have to leave if you don't find those men."

"I'll lead whatever righteous people out of the city with us if we have to leave. Don't worry, I have soldiers out looking already. I'll go out there, myself, too. If there are any out there, we'll find them. If they're not following that prophet Godolfin, that is, which it seems the whole city is now."

"Where will we go?" Lilliana asked, profoundly moved that Ashurta was willing to be their leader amidst all this chaos. Leaving Gomorrah made sense, but where could they go?

"Jehovah will provide a way, but for now we need to find the righteous men of the city to go with us."

"How can we do that while the city is in upheaval?"

"We'll start at the temple, so let's go there now." Ashurta patted her shoulder. "That is, if you're done now."

"I'm ready to go to the temple now. I hope we find some people there claiming sanctuary. We can start with them for the count of the righteous."

"Trust in Jehovah, Lilliana. I know he is new to you, but he has always been there for my people. He won't fail us," Ashurta reassured.

Lilliana called out in her mind to this new Jehovah, hoping that she was truly feeling him in her heart. A new faith was springing inside her, and she prayed silently of her cares.

*** 

The night had fallen and quieted. Eerily so, Lilliana thought, after all the upheaval and rioting that had been happening. Perhaps they would make it safely to the temple after all, although there were still fires burning as they looked out over the main city from the gate of the inner-city. Riding with what few imperial guards were left as well as the remaining Hebrew soldiers, Lilliana hoped they could make it to the temple without being hindered.

The horses hooves clopped against the stonework of the inner-city as they headed to the gate between. The imperial guards at the gate opened it and they passed through. They formed a long caravan heading outward. All were battle ready, just in case. Even Lilliana held her knife in her hand, looking cautiously from side to side.

Riding downhill, they passed a group of onlookers who made as if to challenge them.

"Let us pass, or you'll pay the price," Ashurta called out.

"Give us something," one man called back. "All that we have has been taken."

The moonlight shone on their upturned faces and Lilliana felt her heart go out to them.

"Meet at the temple," she said. "That's where you can go when you're destitute."

"Is that you, High Priestess?" one of them asked.

"Let us pass," Ashurta said again as they began forming a block in front of the horses.

"I'm going to the temple now," Lilliana said. "Follow me there."

"Alright," the apparent leader of the group said at last.

The horses moved forward and Lilliana's tossed its neck as they passed the crowd.

Riding close to Ashurta, she said, "I'm afraid the city is going to be full of them."

"It can't be helped. They've been following that prophet."

"Now that King Birsha has been killed, there'll probably be more following him. The people of Gomorrah are very superstitious about such things. To the victor goes all the success."

"And maybe the spoils," Ashurta mumbled.

"What do you mean?"

"When Godolfin held you captive, did you see any sign of the stolen tribute?"

"I didn't see it," she said. "But I wasn't in more than one house, then that cave."

"But that doesn't mean it wasn't secreted someplace nearby. I have to stop that man. This city is still my responsibility for now."

"I thought you were bent on leaving?" She looked at him under the moonlight.

"The prophecy says the cities of the plain will be destroyed."

"But that was conditional."

"Conditional on whether ten righteous men can be found in any of the cities. If I can find ten here, then Jehovah will spare it. But I don't know about the other cities…"

"And you could remain king. Is that what you want?" she asked, swaying on her mount.

"Godolfin has a stranglehold on this city, and a claim to the throne that may be stronger than mine."

"That depends on whether his illegitimacy is considered superior to your claim. It would take council from all the kings of the cities of the vale to determine it. Their coalition has always made such decisions. Considering what kind of man Godolfin is, I doubt they'll side with him."

The first of the stars overhead began to wink at them. Lilliana looked up at them, wondering if the old gods were still up there or anywhere around them, while she'd begun to believe in this new Jehovah that Ashurta had taught her about. She only wanted to learn more. Her whole life had been spent in spiritual service to the people, and so she wondered if it had all been a waste of time. Yet, a new flicker of hope that Jehovah could get them out of trouble arose within her.

"We've arrived," she said. "I need your help inside gathering the people here for sanctuary."

Dismounting, they entered the temple and the lion Shona ran up to Lilliana.

With a little roar, she appeared to complain.

"Poor Shona," Lilliana cooed. "I bet you're hungry."

"There may be something in the kitchen," Ashurta suggested.

"We may as well start there." Lilliana glanced around, surprised that the temple seemed empty.

Winding down the hall to the back kitchen and its patio, some soldiers followed Lilliana and Ashurta. The kitchen was deserted. But the temple fires were still burning and it was only a few minutes before the guards and soldiers had the torches lit and placed around the temple.

The high priest came barreling around the

corner. He'd ridden over earlier from the palace and he announced, "I found the temple deserted when I got here."

"Where did the staff go? The kitchen workers and the scribes?" Lilliana asked him as he took her hands in his.

"I don't know. I was afraid something might've happened to you, High Priestess," he said, worried.

Extracting her hands, she said, "I'm fine, but I'm afraid Shona has missed her mealtime."

"There'll be a shortage of food throughout the city. Neighbors will have to share with one another. They'll have to help strangers." The high priest clasped his hands and rubbed them absently.

"If they can do that, this city might be spared," Ashurta said. "Charitable acts would be looked upon well by Jehovah. If the city goes that direction, then Jehovah might spare them.

"What is he talking about?" Tamru asked.

"He's referring to the prophecy by the Hebrew prophet Abraham. His God, Jehovah, is threatening to destroy the cities of the vale."

"That is if ten righteous men can't be found," Ashurta qualified.

"What happens if they can't be found in this city? I'm afraid El has deserted the inhabitants and I wouldn't want to see this new Jehovah angry," Tamru said.

"We'll have to leave the city." Ashurta clasped him on the shoulder to reassure the man as he'd started to tremble.

"Where can we go?" Tamru asked.

"If there are enough righteous in one of the other cities, we can go there." Ashurta coughed. "I have soldiers riding out to all of them, and Cousin Lot has gone back to his home in Sodom. He'll contact us later on. We should know by sometime tomorrow."

"And leave this city to its fate, I'm afraid," Lilliana said.

One of the guards interrupted, "High priestess, there are goats still here in the back corral."

"Very good," Lilliana said. "Can you select one of them for the lion's dinner?"

"Yes, High Priestess."

"Good. Then let's see what else we can find here," she said, a little more hopeful that something could be done here at the temple.

They worked all night gathering the supplies remaining in the temple and loading their horses with grain and other food and loading up wagons. They cared for the goats, then secured the corral again. They determined that they'd take Shona and the goats with them if they had to leave the city. With only two imperial guards left, and Tamru the high priest, they only had nine righteous men. If only they could find more.

*** 

At daylight Ashurta led them back to the palace which was bustling with the rest of the Hebrew soldiers who were busy in the kitchen cooking for themselves and the prisoners.

They were just setting down to a meal of boiled barley when Daniel came barging into the dining hall.

"King Ashurta," he said. "King Chedorloamer has been stopped by Abraham's soldiers. They brought back the prisoners and Lot has returned to his city."

"That is fantastic news," Ashurta exclaimed. "What has Prophet Abraham done?"

"He took his army and captured King Chedorloamer's army by night, and they are on their way back to their own country. Their allies won't bother us now, either." Daniel puffed up his chest and grinned.

"You are bringing great news." Ashurta pushed a bowl of barley toward Daniel. "Here, sit and eat." When Daniel complied, Ashurta said, "Perhaps our fortunes are turning for the better now."

The tables in the main hall were full of soldiers returning and mixing with those that had remained all night. It had been a long night of putting down sporadic rebellion and crime all about the city. Ashurta mused that it was what he'd originally come to Gomorrah for, but he'd had no idea what would be entailed. He turned his focus back to his brother as he spoke.

"Well, Chedorloamer has returned to his lands. And the loot he took has been brought back to the city." Daniel chewed energetically.

"Then we should arrange to distribute it –" Ashurta said.

"That won't happen," Daniel said. "The

city's inhabitants have already torn into the wagons carrying the loot. It's been carried off almost as soon as we rode back into the city. I tried to stop them but there were too many of them."

"I'm afraid that is the state of the city now," Ashurta said, his spirits sinking again.

"The prophecy is upon us." Daniel helped himself to a bowl of barley. "The ten righteous men need to be found if we're to stay here."

"I'm in charge of the city now, and I don't think I can find even one more."

"Then we have to leave this place to its doom," Daniel said. "We shouldn't tarry. Abraham didn't say how soon we'd have to leave but we don't want to be caught here when the destruction starts."

"We can't wait to hear back from the other cities and see if they had any luck. Get me fast riders to go to our cousin the king of Zoar. They are closest. We'll stop there, first."

"I'll leave after I eat," Daniel said, and some others listening in at the table volunteered. "We'll know in a day's ride."

"Meanwhile, we need to hunt down that false prophet that's taken over this city." Ashurta finished his barley and pushed his bowl away.

"May your Jehovah have mercy upon us," Tamru said as he entered the dining room.

"Aye, High Priest," Daniel said.

"We shall all pray," Ashurta replied.

They all nodded in silent agreement.

\*\*\*

The city remained in an uprising over the coming days while Ashurta awaited news. He'd sent more riders out to the other cities.

He stood now in the palace garden which was empty of the slaves that had tended it. Without the water running through the channels, the plants were already beginning to wilt in the high heat. If he was staying, he'd have to assign some people to take care of the garden. Right now, as he inspected the petal of a lily that had grown as tall as him, he worried over the state of the city. His new kingdom, for now. He'd left Ur to the hands of the enemies when he'd been compelled to follow his cousin the prophet Abraham. The armies had combined to leave that city and Ashurta couldn't help thinking in hindsight that if they'd stood their ground one more time that they could've restored the city.

Was he leaving Gomorrah now too willingly to follow Abraham again? Would he be able to restore order and peace to the city of Gomorrah if he stood his ground and didn't run off like before? It was different for him now that he was the official leader of the city. The kings of the other cities of the vale would support him in the role. Perhaps they'd find another co-monarch. The city already had a governor to help with it, maybe adding another bloodline ruler would be what the city needed.

What if he didn't follow Abraham this time? What if Jehovah spared the cities? He felt his heart thud in his chest. It was the feeling he got before battle. The sharpness of all his senses piqued. The feel of the wind on his skin a mindful reminder of where he was as it carried the scent of flowers.

He had a decision to make. Abraham had always been his leader, and Jehovah his god, but now he was a king and he had a responsibility to the people of Gomorrah. Straightening, he decided he'd follow Jehovah through the prophet Abraham again. It was all he'd ever known. If it came down to it, that is. If he could find more righteous in this city, he and his army could stay and build a new life for themselves like they hadn't had since Ur. The longing for a home filled him, and he looked back at the palace. His home, for such a short time.

Later that day, he went out among the people with Lilliana to declare that Jehovah would destroy the city.

Despite his being crowned rightfully, he wasn't finding the people receptive. Cries of 'Godolfin' went up around the city here and there. He was unsurprised therefore when the challenge came from the prophet to meet him openly. Word arrived with a messenger who followed Ashurta and Lilliana and then in the marketplace where they had gathered an unhappy crowd, the challenge was called out.

"Godolfin will meet you at the palace before the sun sets," the messenger in red stated.

The crowd cheered, and then it turned into a raucous round of jeering the two of them.

"Who is Godolfin that he thinks he can dictate terms?" Lilliana called out to the messenger who was going along with the crowd.

"He is the new ruler of Gomorrah, a royal commander of the people," the messenger challenged back.

"He ran off last time he faced King Ashurta," Lilliana retorted. She glanced around and saw one of the houses was smoking. "You, there and there," she pointed to the nearest men. "Go check on that house, it's on fire!"

"Why us?" The sweating men peered at the smoke. "Somebody else go there."

"What's wrong with this city?" Lilliana asked the whole crowd.

"I'll send soldiers to handle it," Ashurta said, and signaled her two bodyguards. They loped off in the direction of the smoke.

"Now," Lilliana challenged. "As for this coward, Godolfin –"

The messenger glowered, stomping a foot. "He'll be there when he says, with the force of the people behind him. He is their ruler now. Not this Hebrew."

"I will meet him again," Ashurta shouted back. "But in armed combat again. That is how I'll settle this challenge to my rightful role and stop his taking over the city."

"Ha! You will not dictate terms to King Godolfin. The people have made him ruler, and you will have to accept that." The messenger bounded in place in his fury, punctuating the air with his fists.

"Tell Godolfin that I accept his challenge, and he'd better be prepared to accept mine," Ashurta said as he gathered Lilliana close to him and drew her away from the toxic crowd to lead her back to the palace.

He had preparations to make before

sundown. He intended to win this combat.

# CHAPTER TEN

The sun was beginning to set with its fiery corona lighting up the smoke filled sky. More fires had been started throughout the city and Ashurta had been forced to send out soldiers to put them out. It seemed now as if the entire city had traipsed into the inner-city and surrounded the palace for the showdown. They all awaited.

He heard the chant going up when the prophet arrived before he could see him, "hail, Godolphin!"

He withdrew his sword from its scabbard and planted his feet, ready to meet the other man in combat again. He heaved in a deep breath.

But what met him was a surprise.

The prophet levitated in through the palace entrance while sitting cross-legged and arms outstretched. Ashurta blinked at the hovering man.

The people cheered, and Ashurta felt ire rush through him. This false prophet was displaying the old abilities that had been missing from the royal bloodlines for a very long time. Legends existed still, but here he was.

"My subjects," Godolfin said. "Are here with me."

Ashurta swallowed his surprise and tightly gripped his sword. He'd heard of such things in the faraway East, but it was the first time he'd witnessed levitation. Clearly, the people were impressed.

Recovering, he gripped his sword harder. "I am king now. Descend and fight like the mortal man that you are," Ashurta said.

He looked over to where Lilliana stood gaping at the big prophet hovering in the air. The man looked over at her and leered. Fury filled Ashurta at the man's impudence.

"I am the rightful king here. I am the next in line, and the people support me in my claim to the throne," Godolfin declared, focusing again on Ashurta.

"You are not the legitimate heir to the throne," Ashurta countered. He'd had enough of this wicked prophet. "You've been committing abominations in the name of your power. I know about the human sacrifices and your uprisings. Treason and treachery are what you're guilty of. You will not rule this city."

"You are a stranger in these lands. Who are you to tell us such things?" Godolfin countered, and stretched his legs and settled to stand on them in a defiant stance.

"I am the true king here, and these are my

people now." Ashurta took a step forward. "I've been crowned rightfully, and I know the other kings of the cities of the vale will support me."

"Just look at this crowd. They're following me. They don't believe they are your people. They believe in me. I am in control of the city. Give it up while you still can."

"Let us fight for this throne like tradition declares." Tradition had always held in such challenges, in legends even to wrestling matches to determine kingship. Going back as far as the records, to when the people had still lived in caves, the king had always been the one who was first to rush into battle and the one to protect the tribe. The will to fight coursed in Ashurta's blood.

"I will not fight for what is already mine. I come in peace this day, with the people behind me." Godolfin stood taller, looking down on Ashurta.

"Jehovah will make me the victor. The more powerful god will determine the victory, as is the way of it."

"El is on our side. He's already favored me. I will not fight you for I've already won."

"Draw your sword," Ashurta insisted. He stepped closer with a determined stride when the temple guards suddenly turned on him and faced him with their spears. He looked at them in surprise. "What is this?"

"I am here on a peace mission." Godolfin laughed triumphantly. "And these are my guards now for I'm the new king."

"You aren't a peaceful prophet. You're a false prophet." Ashurta itched for the fight and thought if he goaded the prophet that he'd get a rise. "Come forward now and stand like a man and face me."

"The people believe me and I can do things like I do that show that the gods are with me."

"Jehovah is even greater and if you don't remove yourself from power, Gomorrah will be destroyed by his hand," Ashurta warned.

Godolfin threw his head back in laughter. "This great city can't be destroyed. Not even King Chedorloamer succeeded. You see, he is gone now."

"It's the truth," Lilliana shouted from the sideline. "Lord Ashurta is the new king and Jehovah is the real god. I know it now. You'll be wise to take back your claim to power, Godolfin. Your claim isn't legitimate."

"There now, my sister, you would forsake our gods for one insignificant god of the Hebrews," Godolfin said. Then he smiled wickedly. "You may still be my queen, despite our disagreements."

"I'd never marry you or be your queen." She hissed, "Jehovah has spoken to my heart, something the old gods never did, and I will follow him now."

"So be it." Godolfin lifted his chin and closed his eyes as if in sudden ecstasy and the temple guards removed themselves from behind Ashurta and stepped over to the prophet's side.

"Stand and fight like a man and let the gods decide," Ashurta said. He'd failed to protect Ur from takeover, but maybe he could still protect Gomorrah from this madman. If he could win in combat, the people would have to follow him.

"I've told you once, I come in peace. I'm already the new ruler of Gomorrah. Now, I want you to vacate this palace. I claim it as mine."

"And how do you propose to take it from me?" Ashurta couldn't believe he was helpless again to lose another city to an uprising. Destiny wasn't on his side. He glared at the prophet.

"By the people." Godolfin thrust his fists into the air and a chant went up. The populace was calling out his name. "They stand behind me."

Ashurta muddled over the situation. Anger flared like a red-hot iron with a bellows on it. He couldn't hold off the whole city. A fist settled in his center. He wasn't winning because the false prophet refused to fight. It seemed that Godolfin had truly taken over.

Ashurta was about to try one more tactic but just then, Daniel came bursting in through the entrance pushing past the crowd. He stumbled when he saw the prophet. Then he stepped around him and leapt to Ashurta's side.

"It's time," Daniel said in a hoarse voice. "Lot sends a signal that it's time to leave Gomorrah as soon as possible."

"This is just being decided here, now." Ashurta said.

"It's time," Daniel insisted. "Lot sends word that Abraham's angels have visited him too and told him it is time to flee the cities of the vale."

"Now?"

"Right now. As soon as we can go."

"Where will we go?" Lilliana approached them, overhearing.

Daniel sucked in a deep breath. "King Qayin of Zoar has sent word with his rider. We are welcome there. It seems he's found his ten righteous men and more. The city welcomes us and any refugees from Gomorrah."

"Then the city of Zoar will be spared," Ashurta said, deciding, finally accepting of what was decreed from above. "Come, that is where we will go so we'll leave now."

Ashurta put his sword away and headed out the back of the palace to the sound of cheers erupting from the front of the building. Lilliana and his soldiers were gathering behind him. The supplies were gathered quickly as the palace was being invaded by the surge of supporters of Godolfin.

Ashurta and the others gathered the camels and donkeys and loaded them up, and the onagers with their chariots also holding what supplies they managed to secure. Then they mounted up on the horses in the palace's stables and Ashurta led them to the temple.

Tamru met them and led Shona out on a long leash and said, "I've heard. I'm going with you." He then mounted his own skittish horse. He soothed it and rode up to Ashurta. "We need to take the goats, too."

"My soldiers also know how to herd from the sheep and goats Abraham and Lot brought over with us from Ur," Ashurta reassured him. "We'll take them with us."

A few minutes later, the herd of goats had been gathered and were moving out the city gates along with the horsemen and the caravan. Two of the soldiers walked along beside the goats as they bleated in protest.

Once outside the city walls, Ashurta led the group along the waterway to the south-east onto the road to Zoar. It would be a day before they arrived. Lilliana rode next to him and he reached out and took her hand. She let him and they rode like that for a few yards before dropping her hand back to her pommel.

"Do you think Jehovah will be good to us for leaving?" Lilliana asked. "I had never thought to give up the gods of the city, but my heart believes in this prophecy and Jehovah touched my heart. I didn't like the way the prophet Godolfin took over with the old gods. There is something wrong with him. He is evil and now the city surely is beyond saving."

She talked on further about her hopes and fears while Ashurta listened, smiling in encouragement. Had he ever thought her difficult? Now he wanted to be by her side right where he was.

As they rode, the sky began to darken and distant thunder closed in.

Clouds gathered into a covering like black wool, undulating on a rising wind that whipped their cloth about them. The horses whinnied and the goats cried out in fear.

The sudden change caused Lilliana to glance back over her shoulder at where they'd come from.

"Look up there," Ashurta pointed out. "There is lightning and thunder at Sodom up ahead."

"There is light in the sky over Gomorrah now. Do you see it?" she exclaimed.

"I do now. I think that is Jehovah wreaking his destruction." He gripped the reins tighter.

The earth quaked and Lilliana grasped the horse's neck. The animals let out alarmed cries. Shona's roar topped all of them.

The earth undulated beneath them and the caravan stopped noisily. The landscape rolled on for several minutes as they cowered with nowhere to hide.

After the shaking stopped, the horses settled down again.

A biting hot wind began to blow in earnest.

She cast a glance back at Gomorrah on the back horizon. "Look, it appears to be in flames!"

Ashurta turned in his saddle. "I see it. I know it's Jehovah."

"We got out just in time," Lilliana said. "I think I'll pray to this Jehovah for thanks."

"He has spared us, and now the King of Zoar welcomes us. We'll be able to make a new start there."

"I want a new start with you," she said, then began a prayer in her mind.

"We'll do this together," he said, looking at her intently. "Let's move on. There's nothing we can do now for the residents left behind. Jehovah has spared us."

"I believe in you and this new god," she stated. "I'll follow you as my king and Him as my Lord."

The ground trembled in aftershocks and the sky got even darker from the smoke as they continued to ride.

The caravan rode until nightfall, and broke camp. Lilliana dismounted and saw to Shona the lion while the soldiers tended the mounts and gathered the goats for the night.

They ate dried salted meat and figs and talked of their hopes for a new life away from the wickedness of Gomorrah and the other cities of the vale. Lilliana sat across the fire from Ashurta, but looked up and caught his eye. He looked weary but still smiled back at her.

She rose and moved across the camp to his side. When he made room on a rug for her to sit next to him, she sat. Imploring him, she asked, "is there a place for a high priestess in your religion?"

"There isn't a need for one. You should find something else to occupy your time now," he said gently. "We'll be entering the new royal court as refugees. I'm not certain what I'll do either."

She strained to see him more clearly in the light cast from the fire. "What do you know of the king?"

"Don't you know him?"

"I haven't seen him since I was a teen."

"We should've been able to bring gifts for him. Instead we are dependent upon his good will."

"I wonder if he's changed the temple in Zoar now that he's following Jehovah. I think I'd like to write some hymns to Jehovah. Do you think that will be acceptable?"

"Don't worry so much. Get some sleep,

now," Ashurta urged. "Tomorrow we'll find the answers to all our questions and we'll know our place in the world again.

She nodded and rose and made her bed, with a song in her heart and a prayer on her lips. A new life awaited now, one that included King Ashurta next to her; she could feel it in her heart just as she felt the new Jehovah there now. All would be well again.

# EPILOGUE

*One year later*

Standing next to the king, Lilliana watched from the steps of the palace of Zoar. Striding up to them through the assembled crowd of citizens down below was Ashurta and his lieutenants. His army was in charge of the city and it's peacekeeping. Lilliana felt a swell of love fill her as her gaze locked with Ashurta's.

"My king," he said as he bowed low to the king of Zoar who was clothed in his resplendent golden robe and silver circlet on top of his ginger head. "I've put down the rebellion in the sector that was attacked. All is well again in Zoar."

"Well done, King Ashurta," the king of Zoar replied. "You continue to be a boon to this city."

"I'm proud to serve you, Cousin. May Jehovah continue to watch over you and your family," Ashurta said and straightened.

Reaching out for Lilliana's hand, he took her smaller one in his strong palm and squeezed it in reassurance. She felt the sensation of relief sluice over her that he'd returned home to her after the battle in tact.

Rubbing her pregnant belly with her other hand, she said, "I will always await your return, my husband. Welcome back."

THE END

# AUTHOR'S NOTE

This tale took on a fractured bent when I heard a family tale from a mysterious distant relative who said that there was a legend that the royalty of Gomorrah had escaped. This idea became the backbone of Bitter Fig, and so I've taken the liberty of creating more royalty for Gomorrah. The City of Zoar became the logical place for their end since the Bible stated that that city had been spared. Research on contemporary Canaanites or Kenaani became the basis of the culture of Gomorrah. That, and ideas from contemporary Mesopotamia or Shinar. King Chedorlaomer's kidnapping of Lot was moved to the City of Gomorrah for the sake of storytelling although it's unclear where he was taken.

The approximated timeline of 1867 BCE was selected to reflect other's research into the timing of the events of destruction to Sodom and Gomorrah. It appears to be a time incidental to the prophet Abraham and his travels. The original Biblical story of Sodom and Gomorrah has been expanded upon in that it showed Lot having to scour the City of Sodom for ten righteous men by including that requirement for all the other cities of the Vale of Siddim. It's debated by scholars whether the Canaanites actually performed human sacrifices.

The name of the King of Zoar isn't known; details on the royalty were gleaned from the work of Sir Laurence Gardner. Ashurta and Lilliana are fictional royalty.

# BITTER FIG

## ABOUT THE AUTHOR

Kristin Wall wrote this Biblical historical thriller **Bitter Fig** out of a desire to retell the traditional story of Sodom and Gomorrah from the Bible with a twist from a family tale. She enjoys weaving tales about historical characters and their fictional counterparts for the sake of entertainment. She writes historical fiction from her home in Northern California and has also published a Victorian-era historical novel, *Tear in a Bottle*, and a medieval mystery, *Thorn on a Rose*. The novels are available at Amazon.com.

Made in the USA
Middletown, DE
01 October 2020